Vaulted

LOVERS OF BRANTLEY
BOOK THREE

HAZEL WILDER

Trigger Warnings

This book is a work of fiction, and some material may be triggering for sensitive readers. As an author, I do write about hard topics but try to approach them delicately and with the respect they deserve, without making them too heavy or impactful that they harm the reader. Please read the warnings below and decide if this book will impact your mental health or not. Remember, you are more important than this book, and your mental health matters. Take care of yourself, boo!

- Alcoholism
- Trauma/PTSD
- Panic Attack
- Anxiety
- Profanity
- Abandonment
- Cheating (not the main characters)
- Mention of someone dying at the hands of a SWAT team
- Mention of a side character being in a gang
- Mention of attempted kidnap

If you don't mind the above, turn the page and prepare to be Vaulted.

XOXO,

Hazel

Love in Wrong Places

ASTRID

BEING A TELLER AT THE ONLY BANK IN BRANTLEY IS not for the faint of heart.

Because the bankers? Hot, hot, *hot*.

I watched from afar as Asher talked with the elderly lady I had sent over to him about a loan. It was essential to have a good working relationship with bankers. You could send clients to them and earn referral credits, which kept the managers off your back. When the lady wasn't looking, he gave me a thumbs-up under the table. I grinned. I knew he would close the deal. He always did.

His charm swayed even the most hesitant of clients.

After the lady left, he came up to my window.

"Great work. She also signed up for some life insurance," he told me, his voice low and smoky. He cocked his head at me and lowered his voice further. "Are you busy later?"

I chewed on my lip. I really shouldn't give in again. We had been secretly seeing each other for the last month, and he had promised to break it off with his girlfriend, Chloe, but hadn't yet.

The indecision must've been written on my face because

he leaned forward and whispered, "I'm going to end it tonight. You have my word." He pulled back slightly and looked me over. "Besides, you know what that suit does to me."

I couldn't help the small intake of breath. I did know. He'd told me on our first romp in the sheets that a suit on a woman got him all hot and bothered.

I shook my head. "No. I'm not busy."

His face brightened with an alluring grin. "Good. My place at 8?"

I nodded. I couldn't refuse.

I just hoped he wasn't lying again.

My phone buzzed in my pocket. I waited until break time to look at the message to see it was from one of my best friends in our group chat.

Daisy
Hey! Are you busy tonight?

Astrid
Sorry, just made plans.

Georgia
Tell me you're not seeing Asher again…

Mark
He's bad news. How long has he been telling you he'd break up with his gf, and he still hasn't?

Astrid
Well…

Georgia
Shit…

Rose
And what lie did he tell you THIS time?

Astrid
He said he's going to break up with her tonight.

Daisy
I think this is a really bad idea, Ash... He's been saying that for months.

Astrid
I know. But maybe this time will be different

Rose
I doubt it. You're going to get caught one of these days and rip that poor girl's heart out

Georgia
Why don't you try that new dating app? Maybe you can find someone better on there. Someone SINGLE.

Mark
I concur! You never know who you'll meet on there

I sighed heavily, knowing they were right. I just really liked Asher. He was charming, paid attention to me, and it was so easy to have a conversation with him.

Astrid
I will if he doesn't break up with her tonight. Promise

Daisy
We are just trying to look out for you. You deserve to have someone treat you right

Astrid
Thanks, guys. Talk to you tonight. I'll keep you posted

I slid my phone back into my pocket as a customer came up to my window, my thoughts heavy. It was going to be a long day.

Eight excruciating hours later, I made my way over to Asher's apartment. I didn't see Chloe's Mazda, and hope blossomed in my chest. Maybe he had actually kept his word and broken things off with her this time. My car beeped as I locked it, then made my way up the steps and knocked on the door.

"Hey! Come on in," Asher said as he opened it and pecked me on the cheek.

I took a glance around. Her stuff was still here. I fought the crashing sensation in my body and gave him a tight grin. "I thought you said you were going to break it off with her."

"I am. She hasn't been home yet and is staying late at her shop to finish some stuff."

I shuffled uncomfortably in the doorway. Was this just another of his excuses? "Asher..."

"I don't do things over text. It will be in person. Tonight. I promise." He gave me his charming smile, which melted my heart. "Come in. I'll pop a bottle of wine, and we can relax a bit."

I took a deep breath and followed him, despite my gut telling me to turn around and walk right back out that door. What was I doing? I should be leaving, insisting that he break up with her. Not allowing him to woo me again.

He pressed a wine glass into my hand, then sat on the couch, resting one leg on top of his knee. He had changed out of the suit that he'd worn to work and was now wearing jeans with a white shirt that really brought out his lean but muscular build. He patted the couch next to him.

"Come sit," he commanded.

I glanced around again before obeying, my body tense. He immediately set his wine down and began to rub my shoulders. I wanted to melt into it, but my body was on high alert.

"Geez, you're tense. What's wrong, babe?" he asked.

"I just... It feels like you are making excuses. I don't want to be the mistress, Asher. I'm not a sidepiece," I whispered.

He paused for a moment before continuing to massage my upper back. "I'm not trying to make excuses. I really do plan on breaking up with her tonight. She's just so sensitive that I have to tread carefully and really think about what I'm going to say to her."

I sighed as his lips began to trail along the back of my neck. He gently took the untouched glass of wine from me as his lips moved towards my front, kissing along my collarbone. His hands wrapped around my sides, drawing me closer to him. Our lips connected, gentle and soft, as he began to turn me and lay me down. His hands roamed my sides, igniting my core. My breath started to quicken with anticipation, all thoughts of his girlfriend and the stresses of the day vanishing without a second thought. A breathless moan escaped me as his hand played with a nipple over my shirt.

"Let's go to the bedroom," Asher muttered against my neck, planting another kiss behind my ear.

"Okay," I replied airily.

He stood, then picked me up, crashing his lips to mine again. My arms wrapped around his neck to steady me as he walked us to his room, where he tossed me on the bed. I squealed, followed by laughter, as he jumped in after me, barricading me against the bed with his arms on either side of my head. My insides clenched with expectation.

Our lips met once more, our kisses eager, our tongues

tangoed and tried to assert dominance over the other. Meanwhile, his hand slipped beneath my blouse. I arched my back, allowing him access to undo my bra. It came off quickly, and he began to pull my shirt up, breaking our kiss momentarily as I drew it off of me and threw it aside along with my bra. His warm hand traveled up my curves and to my breast before his mouth was upon my nipple, nipping lightly and sucking on it, drawing moans from me. His other hand began a trail downward, slipping beneath the hem of my pants and resting just above my center. I whimpered and squirmed, trying to get friction.

His mouth disappeared from my nipple, the cold air of the room whispering across it and drawing it taut and hard. His hand withdrew as he leaned back to undo his jeans, watching me with heat in his eyes. Pants went flying, both mine and his, before our lips clashed together again, and his length pressed into my abdomen. I could feel my wetness between my legs. His hand slipped between them and caressed my bud before guiding his cock to my entrance.

"Ready?" he asked breathlessly when he broke away for a moment.

He didn't wait for an answer before thrusting inside me, his balls pressing against my ass. My head fell back, and my fingers gripped onto his shoulders as I moaned loudly, feeling deliciously full. He set a quick rhythm, my insides beginning to clench around him as his thrusting became erratic. He groaned as I ran my fingernails down his back.

"What the fuck?" a woman's voice asked, startling me.

Asher turned, his eyes wide as I screeched and pulled the blankets over me. *Oh no, oh no, oh no.* Chloe stood in the doorway of the bedroom, her eyes wide and hurt. *Nononono.* I had become *that* girl—the girl I didn't want to be.

"Astrid?" she asked as her eyes landed on me.

Fuck.

"Shit. Babe, it's not what it looks like," Asher blurted out.

Babe? But...what...fucking hell. Of course, he'd been lying.

She laughed sarcastically. "I think it's exactly what it looks like." She looked around, spotted my clothes, and tossed them to me. "Get dressed and get the hell out of my apartment."

I nodded quickly, embarrassment heating my cheeks and neck. I rushed into the bathroom, closing the door behind me so I could get dressed. Their arguing could be heard through the door, and I rushed, pulling on my suit and getting out of there as quickly as I could. Chloe was in the kitchen when I exited, pouring herself a glass of wine. My eyes teared up. I felt awful.

"Chloe, I'm so-" I started.

"Just get out," she told me as she pointed to the door.

I nodded and rushed out, not wanting to stay a moment longer. I wanted to disappear into the earth. Once I got to my car, I closed my eyes and allowed the tears to fall. I couldn't imagine what Chloe was going through right now. The betrayal stung for me, but I would think it was worse for her. Taking deep breaths to steady myself, I called Daisy.

"Hey! I thought you were going to be—" she started.

"He lied," I blurted, cutting her off. "She came home and found us in bed together."

"Oh, shit."

Hearing her curse, which she rarely did, only intensified how horrible I felt. I began to hyperventilate.

"Hey. Hey. It's alright. It's not your fault. He's a lying sack of dung," Daisy said.

"Who's that?" I heard Rose ask in the background.

"Astrid," Daisy replied to her twin.

I didn't have to be there to know Rose had an 'I knew it' look on her face. I slumped over and rested my forehead on the steering wheel. "I didn't want to be that girl."

"I know, sweetie, I know. Do you want to come over?"

7

I took a deep breath and let it out. "No. I think I'll go home and drink away my woes."

"Ash..."

"No, I'm okay. Thanks, though, Daisy."

"You know we love and care about you."

"I know."

"Call me if you need me."

I smiled. "Thanks."

"And try that app!" Rose shouted in the background.

I chuckled. "Bye, gals. Talk to you later."

"Later!"

After hanging up, I headed home. My apartment was quiet and cold, lonely—a direct reflection of how I felt. I dropped my purse and keys on the table near the door, then made my way to the kitchen, where I popped open a bottle of wine. Pouring a hefty amount, I carried both bottle and glass back to the living room and plopped down onto the couch.

I thought Asher and I had had something. I had been falling for him, hoping that he would end things with Chloe. Only to end up being the extra. The mistress. The home-wrecker. I hated myself for not listening to my friends and for not seeing through the lies. I should have known better. Sweet words and great sex did not equate to love.

Pulling out my phone, I typed in 'dating apps' to see what came up. Tinder, of course. *No thanks.* Nothing but horndogs there. Bumble, another sex seeking site. Plenty of Fish. *Ah, what's this?* I tapped the screen on some obscure, but well-rated app and read through the reviews.

'Great for people seeking an actual connection, not just sex.'

'Found the love of my life! Thank you so much!'

'Lots of great guys on here!'

'Found my beautiful partner, and we are getting married next month. So glad I downloaded this app!'

Looked promising. I clicked the download button, then spent the next hour working on a profile. It was better than sitting here and wallowing in guilt and pain. After completing the setup, I browsed through some of the men on the app. There were some pretty attractive ones on here, including one with dirty-blond hair and stunning green eyes. I checked his location. *Logan.* Not too far from here, but I wanted someone local. I swiped and landed on an exquisite piece of male creation — dark hair, sparkling dark eyes, tattoos. I bit my lip. *Yummy.* I glanced at his name: Brad. Deciding to go for it, I sent him a wink and a message.

> **Astrid**
> Hey, how's it going?

I set my phone down, not expecting much to come out of it right now. It was almost ten at night after all, and most good citizens were in bed by now, especially if they had to work the next day.

Shit.

Work.

I would have to face Asher again tomorrow. I groaned. Hopefully, he would know better than to try to approach me after the fiasco that was tonight. What would I even say to him if he did try to come up to me? I couldn't be weak anymore, that was for sure. I would need to be somehow stronger than his alluring personality.

My phone chimed and pulled me from my thoughts. Glancing down, I saw a notification from the app I had downloaded. Quirking a brow, I pulled it up and saw a response from Brad.

Brad
Well, hello there, beautiful. Nm. Haven't seen you on here before

Astrid
Nah, just downloaded it. Thought I'd give it a go

Brad
Well, lucky me!

I blinked at his quick response. This could get interesting.

Brad
What made you want to message me out of all the fish in the sea?

I smiled. That was a cute way of putting it. I paused. Really, my first thought had been how attractive he was. I took the initiative to look at his profile. He liked hiking, fishing, and bowling. His favorite color was blue, and he was very proud of his truck. Personality? Easy-going, down-to-earth, and looking for a girl to spend time with. Not a lot of information to go off of, but that was alright with me.

Astrid
Well, you describe yourself as easy-going. I'm curious how true that is. You know how these apps go. You can hide behind a screen too easily.

Brad
Ouch! You wound me.

Astrid
Sorry to be too blunt

Brad
Haha! I was teasing. I'd like to think that I'm pretty easy-going. I prefer to live stress-free, low drama

Astrid
Well, that's what made me want to message you. What made you message back?

The typing icon came up a few times, and I chewed on my lip nervously. This is why I didn't like dating apps. You couldn't read someone's body language through a screen. He could be a creepy older man for all I knew. He could also be lying.

Brad
You look friendly. Kind. And your bio says about as much

I smiled. That was sweet.

Astrid
Well, thank you

Brad
So... what do you do?

Astrid
I'm a bank teller

Brad
At Central Bank?

Astrid
Well, I don't know of any other banks here in Brantley...

Brad
Lol me either. That's cool. Do you like it?

> **Astrid**
> Most days. I definitely have some favorite customers. What do you do?

> **Brad**
> Construction. I'm actually working on a project down the road from your work right now. Maybe I could swing by sometime, and we could grab a bite?

I paused. That was fast... Was it too fast? I wasn't too sure. What was the normal time frame when people would meet up?

> **Brad**
> I mean... only if you want to

> **Astrid**
> Sure, that would be nice

> **Brad**
> Sweet. Well, I'm headed to bed. Chat tomorrow?

> **Astrid**
> Okay 🙂

Now I would just have to wait and see how this went. I felt hopeful, but I was also still on edge after Asher. I had my doubts about Brad's genuineness, which is something I always struggled with when trying online platforms. I'd tried them before, but my criticality got the best of me, and they never went anywhere. I'm sure some guys would have been really great, but I was my own worst enemy. I would give Brad the benefit of the doubt. He seemed really nice. *But so does everyone online.*

The next day, I woke with trepidation about the day. Asher would be there, and I would have to face him. Now I understood why they say never to date anyone where you work. I pulled into the parking lot and slipped inside, thankfully unnoticed. It was a Friday, so it would be plenty busy. Hopefully, that meant that I would have little to no interaction with him.

I wasn't so lucky.

Lunch time rolled around, and as I made my way into the break room, Asher was there. He looked up as I entered and gave me his usual charming grin. Now it just made my stomach turn in knots. *Not* in a good way.

"Hey," he greeted. "I was hoping to catch you."

"I'm good," I blurted out and tried to make a beeline for the women's restroom.

He blocked my path. "Look, I'm sorry about what happened last night."

"Okay." I tried to go around him.

"Are you upset?"

My brows furrowed as I blinked. Was he serious? "Am I upset?"

He nodded, a look of fake concern coming over his face. How had I not noticed it before? This acting. This game he was playing.

"Am I *upset*?" I asked again through gritted teeth and fought to keep my voice down. "Of course I'm *upset*! You *promised* me that you would break up with her, but you didn't. For *months*. Then she finds us *in bed* together, and you want to ask me if I'm *upset*?"

He tried to reach for me, but I backed up.

"Don't. I want nothing to do with you anymore, Asher. Just leave me alone."

His eyes narrowed. "Fine. Be a bitch about it."

I scoffed, completely taken aback by his words.

"Just know that you're missing out," he seethed as he stormed away.

"Yeah, not much," I muttered.

He left me alone the rest of the day. If it continued like that, I would be thankful that this had happened the way it did. At least he was handling it maturely. It would be awful if he went to the manager about it. I couldn't afford to switch locations to the next town over. The commute would kill my savings plan and make it harder to afford things than they already were as a single woman.

"Hello, beautiful," a deep voice startled me from my thoughts.

A man stood at my window in a dirty t-shirt and Carhartt jeans. He looked fresh off the construction field. It took me a moment to recognize him, and I blinked a few times to gather my thoughts.

"Brad?" I asked.

He nodded, giving me a bashful smile. "I'm sorry to bother you at work. I just really wanted to meet you in person, and I just got on my lunch break, so I thought I would swing by. Hope that's alright."

My heart flopped. I was both endeared and concerned. It felt like this was moving faster than I expected. "Yeah, no, that's fine. I just..." I laughed awkwardly. "You caught me off guard."

"Sorry about that." He paused as if to think. "Are you going on break soon?"

I shook my head. "No, I already took my lunch. I don't get off till five."

He grinned. "Oh, great. Maybe we could grab dinner then?"

I flushed. "Uh, yeah. Sure."

"Great! I'll meet you back here, then we can go wherever you'd like."

"Okay."

He tapped the counter. "Cool. Well, later."

"Later."

I watched him walk away, not bothering to keep my eyes from ogling his muscles and confident walk. Warning bells pealed in my mind annoyingly.

"Hey, Mark," I called over to my coworker.

He peeled his eyes off Brad's backside and raised a brow. "Yeah?"

"I'm going to run to the back really quick."

He nodded. "When you get back, I want a rundown on *that*." He motioned with his hand in the direction that Brad had taken.

I laughed and locked up before heading to the break room. I pulled out my phone as soon as I got into a bathroom stall.

> **Astrid**
> Hey. How fast is TOO fast on those dating apps?

> **Georgia**
> What do you mean?

> **Rose**
> Did you already find someone?!

> **Astrid**
> So... I talked to this guy last night. And then he showed up here and asked me to dinner tonight. We didn't even talk that much.

Georgia
Girl...

Rose
That screams red flag

Georgia
Or maybe he's just lonely! I say give him a chance

Daisy
I agree with Georgia. If nothing else, to get your mind off of Asher

Astrid
Alright... I'll text you the place we'll go and when I'm done

Rose
Stay safe!

Later that day, I waited by my car after helping lock up and close down the bank. It was fifteen after, and I was getting ready to leave when a large truck drove up. I shifted, prepared to get in my car, when it parked next to me, and Brad stepped out.

"Hey! Sorry, I'm a bit late. Some guys needed help," he told me. "How was your day?"

"It was long," I told him honestly. "But it was good."

"That's good to hear. Where would you like to go?"

"How about Mariposa?"

"Sounds great." He smiled widely. "Do you want to meet there or do you want to carpool in my truck?"

I found myself relaxing. He was so sweet already and like a breath of fresh air. "We can carpool."

That seemed to make his smile brighter. He followed me around his truck, then opened the door for me before helping me in. My heart swooned. No guy had ever done that for me before. The engine revved loudly as he made his way back onto the main streets to head down Main Street toward the restaurant. As he drove, I shot a quick text to my friends to let them know where we were going. Could never be too safe.

"So what was the highlight of your day?" he asked.

"I'm sorry?" I was confused by what he meant. No one had ever asked that.

He chuckled. "Meaning, what was your favorite part of the day?"

"Oh!" I laughed at myself. "Uh, well, I guess helping my favorite customer. She likes to tell me these wild stories every time she comes in. I'm not sure how true they are, but she tells them as if she believes them to be. Today's story was about a neighbor's goat terrorizing her chickens."

"Sounds like an interesting tale!"

I shrugged. "It was amusing. What about you?"

"Hm, I'm not really sure. It was pretty monotonous. Just laying down concrete and making sure it sets right."

"Oh. That sounds..."

"Don't say interesting. It's boring as fuck."

I laughed. "Okay, I won't."

As soon as we parked at Mariposa, he went around the truck to get the door for me, but I had already opened it. He chuckled.

"I take it you haven't met a chivalrous man before," he commented.

"Why do you say that?" I asked.

"Well, I was raised to always open the door for a lady." He grinned. "You seemed surprised the first time, and this time you opened it yourself."

I blushed. "Yes, you would be right. I'm not used to that."

"That's alright. Will you at least let me get the door at the restaurant?" His eyes sparkled with humor.

I chuckled. "Yes, sir."

He winked and led me inside, gently placing a hand on my lower back. I was a little shocked at the touch, but it also sent butterflies fluttering in my stomach. As soon as we sat down to order, I took the time to admire him a little more discreetly. He was tan, probably from spending all day in the sun. Muscles corded down his arms. Tattoos trailed from shoulder to hand. That's when I noticed it.

A pale band around his ring finger on his left hand.

My stomach dropped, and my guard went up.

His eyes caught mine, and I quickly looked away, focusing on the menu instead.

"What looks good to you?" he asked as he set his menu down.

"Hm, I think the taco salad looks pretty good," I replied as casually as I could.

He cocked his head slightly. "Everything alright? You look a little pale."

"Yeah, yeah. I, uh..." I decided to go with honesty and slowly let out a breath. "I just caught sight of your hand."

He lifted his right hand. "Oh, the scar?"

"No, no. Your left hand."

He dropped his hand and looked down. "Oh, that."

An awkward silence stretched between us.

"We are separated. Have been for a few months now," he finally said quietly.

I blinked. I hadn't expected that. I wasn't really too sure what to think. Or how to react.

"I understand if you don't feel comfortable continuing." His dark eyes met mine again, practically pleading for me to understand.

"Why?"

"Well, I wouldn't want you to—"

"No." I shook my head. "I mean, why did you separate?"

"That's a bit hard to explain..."

I waited for him to expound, but he didn't. I took a deep breath. If he couldn't explain it, how did I know if he was telling the truth? I should have known this was too good to be true.

"Right," I finally said and began to grab my purse. "Look, I think you are lovely, but I'm not going to go down this road again. If, and when, you get it finalized, I wish you the best, but I don't think this is going to work."

"Wait, Astrid, please."

I shook my head and stood, making a beeline for the exit. Nope. Not going to happen. I called a cab to take me to my car, then went home.

concluded a month ago that I needed to change it. Needed to move away. It was the only thing that was holding me back from healing and moving on. So it was time to put some distance between myself and this place. Time to dream new dreams and make new memories in a fresh place. One that wasn't tainted.

With a sigh, I pulled the door closed behind me and turned the key. The finality of the sound seemed to travel throughout my body, down to the very marrow of my bones. I placed the key in the key box the realtor had placed around the doorknob yesterday, then ambled down the sidewalk to my truck. As I walked past the "For Sale" sign, I took a deep breath and tried to put a lively pep in my step. It was false. But for Sophia's sake, I needed to pretend that all was right in the world. Pretend that I was making a fully informed decision and not one to escape the ghosts that threatened to consume me.

I slipped into the driver's seat of my truck and smiled at her in the back seat. "Ready to go, kiddo?"

Her brown eyes peered back at me from her six-year-old face, curious and slightly afraid. "Do we *have* to move, Daddy?"

My heart squeezed. This place was all she had known. "Yes, sweetheart, we do. But we are going to a better house. One that has a fenced-in backyard and a pool."

She smiled, but it didn't meet her eyes, which began to water. "What about Mommy? Will Mommy be there?"

I tried to hide my wince. "No, honey. Remember what I told you? That Mommy moved somewhere else, so we have to move, too?"

"To be closer to her?"

I smiled sadly. "No."

She sniffled. "But I like *this* house."

"I know."

All the Same

ETHAN

THE DAY HAD COME. EVERYTHING WAS PACKED away, and I turned around in my now-empty house, making sure nothing had been forgotten. The pictures that had once hung on the walls had vanished, leaving empty dust-bordered whiteness in their stead. The decorations, knick-knacks, and memories had been packed into neat little boxes, leaving the echoes of their existence in the dust upon the mantle. The living room in which I stood was hollow, and every movement was loud as though it could fill the vacancy with the noises of shuffling clothing and feet upon the hardwood floor that had once boomed with laughter and joy. My heart ached in my chest.

It was time to move on from here. Away from this place where I had thought everything in life was going right. That I had finally made it. A place I thought I could settle down, fill this home with the love of my little family, and have peace. I had been wrong.

For a year, I tried to stay here. Tried to make it work. Counseling and therapy couldn't erase the pain this house caused each time I walked through the door. I finally

I turned away from her, trying to keep from breaking down. I didn't know how to handle this. Didn't know how to explain to her that her mother had decided to leave us. Had abandoned her. I didn't want her to feel like it was her fault, because it wasn't. Anger and grief swirled in my gut, a toxic combination that I had no clue how to handle.

"Can we still get a puppy?" Sophia asked suddenly, her voice choked up.

I glanced at her in the mirror. She was trying to be strong. "Of course. Any puppy you want. And you can paint your room any color."

"Even bubble-gum pink?"

I nodded as I turned the engine over and began to make my way to Brantley. It was only an hour drive, but it was far enough away that I could forget everything behind us, far enough that we could move on and make life better for us.

The new house was smaller, but had a large yard, as I had promised, and a pool in the backyard. I had picked it solely for that reason, knowing how much Sophia loved the water. I let her see her room, then we went to Lowe's to get some paint for it. That evening, we painted her room and ate pizza. Her laughter filled my soul, making it feel lighter despite the circumstances. She fell asleep in a bundle of blankets on my bed, her face peaceful. I turned off the lights with a sad smile.

"I promise things will look up from here," I whispered to her before retiring to the living room couch.

I only hoped that I could keep it.

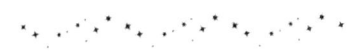

In the months after our divorce, I had tried to plead with

my ex-wife, for Sophia's good if nothing else, but she had made it clear that she wanted nothing to do with either of us. She would rather go party and drink with her lowlife friends than commit to our relationship and daughter. It had hurt, but I had seen it coming for months. I only wanted her in Sophia's life so she would have a mother, but I knew it was a useless battle.

I tried to date after the divorce was finalized. I waited for six months, letting myself heal and come to terms with how life would be from here on out. All the women of Logan were like my ex-wife. None of them wanted to be tied down, didn't want to be the mother of a child. Especially one that wasn't even theirs to begin with. Maybe Brantley would be different. I hoped that women there would be more mature and ready to settle down. Now that I was here, I would try again.

I got on the dating app I had downloaded a week ago and browsed through it. One woman in particular caught my eye. She had a kind face and sparkling brown eyes. Her blonde hair was whispering across her face in her picture as she looked back at the camera, laughing. She glowed with joy. I clicked on her profile, hope blossoming in my chest for the first time in months, and began to swipe through her pictures. There were pictures of her and what I assumed were her friends, her riding a horse, and one with... Ugh. Her drinking at a nightclub with her friends.

I sighed and exited, moving on to the next. A pretty brunette with emerald eyes smiled at me from my screen. Her photos showed her reading, hiking, and cuddling with a dog. Under her profile, she had marked "No" for drinking and smoking. I grinned. That was more like it.

Ethan
Hello. How are you doing this evening?

A few minutes later, she responded.

> **Naomi**
> Good. How are you?

> **Ethan**
> Pretty good. Just settling in for the night.

Come on, Ethan. That was lame, I chided myself and started typing again.

> **Ethan**
> I see you like to read. What was your latest book?

I mentally patted myself on the back. Good save.

> **Naomi**
> Well, I'm currently reading The Hobbit for the fourth time.

Oh. She was *that* kind of a reader. Not that there was anything wrong with it, but in my experience, it could go one of two ways: she was either going to be super anxious or super nerdy. I hated to judge a person by their tastes, but I could only go by experience.

> **Ethan**
> Oh, wow. I haven't taken those on yet, but I liked the movies.

> **Naomi**
> Yeah, they are nothing like the books!

> **Ethan**
> So I have heard. But what movie is that's based on a book?

Naomi
True!

Ethan
I actually just moved here from Logan.
Know of any good places to grab dinner?

Naomi
Well, we have Mariposa, a Latin family
restaurant popular with locals. There's also
Bob's Grill, if you're looking for a good
steak. If you want Italian, we have Gusto
Italiano.

Ethan
What do you prefer?

Naomi
Depends on the day, but you can never go
wrong with Mariposa.

Ethan
Would you want to meet me there on
Saturday? I prefer to meet face-to-face, if
that's alright with you.

Naomi
Sure! I know what you mean. People can
pretend to be whoever they want online, but
in person, it is much harder. What time?

Ethan
6?

Naomi
Great. I'll be there.

I smiled. Now I just had to find a babysitter. I hopped
onto the app I used to find sitters in the past and messaged

Sophia's favorite: Leora. Thankfully, she was available and willing to make the drive for an extra twenty dollars.

Saturday night arrived, and I grew more anxious as the evening approached.

"When will you be home?" Sophia asked me.

"After you go to bed, but I will come in and give you a kiss when I get back," I reminded her for the umpteenth time.

"Can Leora get ice cream?"

"There's already ice cream in the freezer."

The doorbell rang, and Sophia ran to get the door.

"Don't answer the door without—" I started as I followed her.

"LEORA!" Sophia's excited squeal cut me off.

I sighed and gave Leora a tight smile. "Hey. Thank you for driving all the way out here."

"Of course! I would've brought Michael with me so they could play, but he caught a cold at school," she explained.

"No problem. I'm sure Sophia will have fun regardless." I shook her shoulder gently for emphasis.

"Yep!" She grabbed onto Leora's hand. "Come on! Let me show you my new room. It's pink!"

She chuckled as she was being pulled away.

"Thank you!" I called after her. "I'll be back by eight at the latest!"

Leora's thumbs-up popped out of Sophia's doorway.

I laughed as I went to my truck and started down the road. Pulling into Mariposa, I wasn't sure what I had expected, but it definitely was a lot more crowded than I had anticipated.

Walking into the restaurant, I was taken aback by all the colors and plants. It felt lively and welcoming.

"Hi, Ethan?" a woman approached me, her emerald eyes shining.

"Naomi, hi," I greeted with a smile. "Thanks for meeting me. This place is amazing. I feel like I traveled to South America."

She giggled. "The owners are Venezuelan-American, so I'm not surprised."

A hostess quickly led us to our seats, and I took the time to look around. Plants of all shapes and sizes were *everywhere*. It felt like I had stepped into an oasis, and I understood why it was a favorite.

"*Hola*, welcome to Mariposa. Can I start any appetizers for you?" a young woman asked, her accent thick.

I quirked a brow at Naomi. "Would you like anything?"

She shook her head and placed her menu down. "No, I'm okay with just the entree."

The waitress nodded. "Are you ready? Or do you need a few more moments?"

We placed our orders, then silence fell upon us. I wasn't sure what to say first.

"So what brought you to Brantley?" Naomi asked.

I breathed a quiet sigh of relief. Conversation was complicated for me when it came to dating. "I needed a change of scenery. There was a lot of... memories tied to Logan that I needed to get away from so I could move forward."

Her brow quirked up, and she sat a little straighter. "Nothing horrible, I hope."

I chuckled and shook my head. "Not unless you count an ex-wife."

"Ah, I'm sorry." She winced in sympathy.

"Nothing to be sorry for. It's for the best for my daughter and me."

"Oh. You have a daughter?"

I tried to gauge her reaction as I nodded. "Yes, she's six."

"So young! Poor thing. Is her mother involved at all?"

I shook my head. "No."

Naomi sighed. "That's just awful."

The conversation flowed easily for the rest of the meal. I could feel myself growing lighter. Maybe it would be different this time around.

"Thank you for dinner, Ethan," Naomi said after I walked her to her car.

"Thank you for your recommendation. It was delicious," I replied.

She grinned before sliding into her driver's seat.

As promised, I kissed Sophia's head when I got home, and she didn't even stir. I smiled down at her, then went to my room and plugged my phone in to charge. A notification from the app glared at me as it lit up. Curious, I opened it and found a message from Naomi.

> **Naomi**
> Hi, Ethan. I wanted to say thank you again for dinner. Unfortunately, I don't think we should continue pursuing anything. I wish you the best.

I sighed, feeling the hope that had blossomed in my chest come crashing down. I guess Brantley wouldn't be much different after all.

The New Banker

ASTRID

THE ALARM'S LOUD BEEPING WOKE ME FROM A DEEP sleep. With a groan, I swung my arm over and smacked it to turn it off. Mondays were always the worst. I didn't know why, but it seemed to be a social consensus that I agreed with. Society really did need a three-day weekend, not just two.

I rolled out of bed and rubbed at my eyes. With a yawn, I pulled myself to standing, sliding into my slippers and making my way to the bathroom. A hot shower helped to wake me, but I eagerly waited by the coffee pot while it brewed. Feeling like I needed to move to stay awake, I went back to the bedroom and stood in front of my closet, trying to decide what to wear. *I should update my closet this weekend*, I thought absently as I took in all the women's suits I had purchased, only to draw the attention of Asher. I rolled my eyes at myself. I had been so stupid.

I settled on a cute black sweater and a gray pencil skirt. It was getting cold out, and this could be perfect for the cooler weather. I paired it with some knee-high socks and black leather boots. I frowned. I wasn't going to a funeral. I needed a color pop. Crossing over to my standing mirror, I pulled it open to take a look at what I had for jewelry. It had been a while since I had worn any. I pulled out some red leather leaf earrings and a matching black-and-red beaded necklace with a red leather leaf dangling from the center. I slipped on some plain silver chains to accentuate the necklace and add some variety. Then I pulled back a small section on both sides of my head and snapped it in place with a red bow.

Closing the mirror, I rechecked my outfit and nodded, satisfied with the way I looked. Beeping drew my attention, and as I entered the kitchen, the sweet, roasted aroma of brewed coffee perked me right up. I poured in some creamer, then turned to lean against the counter, both hands wrapped around the mug as I tilted it slightly to take a sip. Hot liquid seared my tongue slightly as I savored the flavor with closed eyes.

"Much better," I commented to myself, taking another sip.

Then I slipped the lid on and made my way out the door, making sure to lock it behind me.

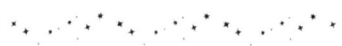

I walked into the bank with new confidence and slipped into the vault to grab my box, then into my teller station, where I started up the computer. It was typically slow, so while it booted up, I began putting in my cash station.

"Have you seen the new banker yet?" Mark whispered from behind me.

I glanced over at him and shook my head. Today, he was

wearing a flamboyant pink shirt with a dark black vest and pants. His pierced brow quirked up as he nodded in the direction of the lobby. Diverting my attention, I peered into the banker's area, where I could see a man setting up his desk. He had sandy blond hair and wore a brown suit with black loafers. From the way his suit stretched taut as he reached down to boot up his computer, I knew he would be muscular. He placed pictures next to his computer, and when he looked up, I quickly looked away so I wouldn't be caught.

"From what I see, he looks like any other banker," I told Mark.

"Wait till you see his eyes," he said wistfully.

"Well, if you find him so attractive, why aren't you introducing yourself?"

Mark quirked a brow at me. "That man is as straight as an arrow, Astrid." He waved a hand at me. "You would have much better luck at tapping that than I would wearing a Sunday hat on a Tuesday."

I chuckled and shook my head.

"Besides, I had a date this weekend, and he was *fine*."

"I'm sure you'll be telling me all about it today."

"Damn right I will." He hip-checked me. "Now don't be too shy with that new banker. He looks right up your alley, and I hear he's single." He slipped into his station next to mine.

I shook my head. "I'm thinking of giving dating a break for a while."

He gasped dramatically, making me chuckle. "Now, why on earth would a goddess like you say that?"

"Men are tools and cheaters. The whole lot of 'em."

He snorted. "Well, I take offense to that."

I simpered. "Except you, of course." I sighed heavily. "I had an awful date over the weekend. He was super sweet, and I was really hoping he would be good, but when we got to the restaurant, he had a tan line."

Mark gasped again for a completely different reason and leaned over the barrier. "What?! He was married?!"

"He claimed they were separated, but I just am having a hard time trusting that after..." I looked away.

He winced. "Oh, yeah. *That*. I don't blame you, girl."

"Anyways, tell me about *your* date this weekend."

He pulled away from the barrier, his body language showing his excitement. "When I say he was fine, mm," he started, closing his eyes and putting a hand over his heart.

I giggled.

"He had dark hair, dark eyes, and *muscles*. And the boy knew how to use his—"

"Alright, that's enough gossip, you two. You need to get the meeting," our lead teller, Helen, interrupted, a smile blooming across her face.

I groaned inwardly but nodded. "Be right there."

I locked up and followed Mark to the daily morning meeting. It was boring, as usual, and completely useless. Team building here was a joke. We already knew who to trust and who not, who to refer to or direct to customers. We didn't need team-building exercises for that. I made sure to avoid Asher like the plague. I really did need to find a new coworker to refer to now that I would be steering clear of him.

Glancing over at the new banker, I realized I recognized him. But from where? I searched my memory, then it hit me. He had been on that dating app, but had been living in Logan. Or at least, that's what his profile had said. Had he traveled an hour just to work here? I doubted it. It was more likely that he had moved here. What were the chances of that? I would have to do some snooping on my break.

The hours ticked by slowly. Mondays were always sluggish as most people got paid on Fridays and had spent their money over the weekend. The only thing lively was Mark, and the rest of the mindless chatter from my other coworkers.

"I cannot wait for the weekend," Mark sighed next to me.

"Are you going to see him again?" I asked nonchalantly as I doodled on a sticky note.

"Of course! I'm going to let this one run its course. Maybe it'll last a while."

I sat up and peered over at him. "Uh-oh."

He perked up immediately, looking around for something amiss before turning to me with a question on his face. "What?"

"You look smitten!"

He waved a hand at me. "Pish posh. You know not of what you speak."

I laughed. "You are *so* smitten by him, Mark! You look like a forlorn puppy waiting for its owner to come home."

"Shut up." His cheeks turned pink.

Oh, he had it bad, alright. I smiled. "I'm happy for you. At least one of us is getting lucky."

"You'll have your run of it soon enough. Bad luck can't last forever."

I shrugged and went back to doodling. "Perhaps."

"Maybe with a certain banker?"

I blinked. "Uh, no. I think I will pass on that. It's bad enough still having to work with Asher."

"You do have a point." He sucked on his teeth. "I'm assuming you're trying that dating app Georgia is always raving about?"

I nodded. "That's how I met Brad." I lowered my voice and leaned closer to the barrier, Mark copying my movement. "And the new banker is on there, too."

His eyes went wide, and a sly smile appeared on his face. 'Told you he was single."

"Yeah, but I'm not dating coworkers again. It would make

life miserable if I had to deal with *both* of them here. Can you imagine?"

"Well, Asher doesn't strike me as the jealous type, but I could be wrong. However, I could see how that would make work...tense." Mark paused and looked over at the bankers' area. "I don't know. Could make work interesting, too."

I snorted. "I'm not going to do it just for your entertainment."

He made a show of pouting before we collapsed into giggles. Once we caught our breath, he wiped away tears that had escaped.

"Red alert. Incoming bad date," Mark whispered as he leaned away.

I looked up to see Brad coming towards my station. His handsome face looked determined. My stomach sank as my heart began to race with anxiety. I shook my head at him, hoping he would turn around and walk away, but he didn't. I locked up my drawers and computer before he got to my window.

"Astrid, please," he said quietly. "Give me a chance to explain."

"You have nothing to say that I want to hear," I whispered. "Please leave."

"My wife and I are separated. We have been for months. We have fallen apart over the years and become strangers, and we agreed that we can start seeing other people." His voice was urgent, pleading.

"I don't care. I don't want anything to do with it."

"Astrid—"

"She said she's not interested, man," Mark leaned over to say.

"This doesn't concern you," Brad snipped.

"Brad, you need to leave. This is my place of work," I urged.

"Is there a problem here?" Asher asked as he approached us.

"This...gentleman," Mark began, practically spitting the word, "is bothering our dearest Astrid and won't take no for an answer."

Asher glanced between us, and I wanted to sink into the earth beneath me. He nodded once.

"It's time for you to go, sir," Asher said as he moved to place his body between my station and Brad.

Brad looked him up and down, sizing him up, before glancing over his shoulder at me. "Fine."

"And don't bother her again," Mark added.

Brad nodded once before turning and walking back out the door. I breathed a sigh of relief that was quickly doused when Asher turned around.

"What was that about?" he asked, a brow quirking up.

"Nothing that concerns you," I whispered.

"Are you dating him?"

"It's none of your business who I decide to date, but in answer to your question, we went on *one* very short date."

His eyes narrowed. "Astrid, I care—"

"Don't you dare say you care about me. I appreciate you stepping in, but I have no desire to rekindle anything between us. I think it's best if we just keep it to work relations only."

"Very well. Make sure you keep your boyfriends out of here if you want to keep work and life separate."

"Is that a threat?" I blinked in surprise.

"Let's just say, you should be glad I don't tell Helen about this." Then he stormed back to his desk.

Mark scoffed. "Unbelievable. I guess he *is* the jealous type."

"Guess so," I muttered and sat down on my stool.

Life had suddenly gotten so complicated. I should have listened to my friends a long time ago and broken things off with Asher sooner. I wasn't sure why he thought he could lay some claim on me. I had never truly been his to begin with. He had seen to that when he had strung me along for the last several months. He had no place to act jealous when he had been dating another woman while telling me he cared for me. It was all just more of his lies and manipulation. I wouldn't fall for it.

"Helen wouldn't do anything about it, you know," Mark interrupted my thoughts.

I looked up and quirked a brow. "What do you mean?"

"Meaning, she would just back you if some guy were to give you trouble. She knows we have lives outside of work, and sometimes life gets messy. So long as customers aren't impacted, which they weren't, you're good. But *if* anything like this should happen again, maybe take it to the break room. I'll cover for you so you can deal with your stuff."

I smiled, my heart warming. "Thanks, Mark. You're the best."

"And you know it." He winked at me.

I laughed, glad I had a friend like him to have my back when I needed it most.

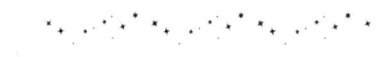

My lunch break rolled around about an hour later, and I gratefully locked up before making my way to the back. My mind full of whirring thoughts, I wasn't paying attention to my surroundings when I swung open the break room door and walked in, colliding with something hard. Hot liquid poured down my shirt, making me gasp and step back in shock as I looked down. The smell of coffee wafted to my nose.

"Holy shit! Are you okay?" a man asked.

Strong hands rushed out toward me, dabbing me with napkins. I grabbed them from him and began wiping the coffee from my sweater as best I could. *Well, this alters my plans slightly*, I thought as I glanced up into the concerned forest green eyes of the new banker.

"I'm alright. Though I think my skirt would say otherwise," I chuckled as I glanced down to see the coffee stain spreading across the front of me.

"I'm so sorry. I didn't see you coming in and—"

"It's alright. Accidents happen." I gave him a shy smile.

He was even more handsome up close than the pictures online had shown. His green eyes had flecks of gold in them that drew me in. A strong jawline flexed nervously before he smiled softly in embarrassment.

"Well, this is an awful way to introduce myself, but I'm Ethan," he said, his voice deep.

It had my insides clenching. *No. No*, I chided myself. *We agreed not to be attracted to anyone from work. Work and life shouldn't mix.* He quirked a brow when I didn't immediately respond, and my cheeks flushed as I tried to recover myself quickly.

"Sorry. Astrid," I replied, holding out my hand.

He took my offered hand, and a bolt of electricity shot through me upon impact, making my core clench again. I was so fucked.

"Nice to meet you, Astrid," he said quietly, then his eyes narrowed. "Have we met before?"

Oh, no. He must have seen me on the app, too. "Uh, no. I don't think so." I pushed some hair behind my ear.

"Strange. You look familiar. Have you ever visited Logan before?"

I shook my head. "No. I usually stay close to home."

"Hm." He shrugged. "Well, in any case. I'm sorry again for

spilling coffee on you. Do you need a ride somewhere to get that out?"

"No, no. That's alright. I was going to go home for lunch anyway."

"Oh, good." He laughed nervously. "I see. Well, again. I am so sorry."

I shrugged. "Things happen. I need to get going, though. It was nice meeting you."

"You too."

I grabbed my purse and rushed out the door, completely embarrassed and, strangely, turned on. He had caught me by complete surprise in my attraction to him. What was it about men in suits that drew me in? Though thinking back, it wasn't even him in a suit. It was just *him*. His eyes, his hands, his face... I shivered as desire coursed through me.

I was going to have to be very careful around him, or I might find myself falling.

"Um, excuse me. Since when did you decide to start changing outfits midway through the day?" Mark asked as I came back in from taking my break.

"I had a run-in with the new banker," I said, trying to sound nonchalant.

He gasped. "Do tell!"

I chuckled. "Well, when I went in the back, we kind of... collided. He spilled his coffee on me."

"Oh my! How romantic."

I scoffed and gave him some side eye. "So while I was home, I got changed."

"And?"

"And what?"

"Well, what did he say?!"

"He apologized and introduced himself."

He groaned. "That's it?"

I nodded.

"Oh. Incoming." He quickly turned away.

"Hey," a familiar deep voice greeted, and I looked up to see Ethan standing in front of me at my window. "Glad you had time to run home and change. I wanted to apologize again."

I felt my cheeks grow hot. "That's alright. It was an accident. Were you able to get more coffee?"

He grinned with a nod and held up a travel mug. "Made sure to put the lid on this time."

I giggled. "Good call. Unless that's how you normally introduce yourself to tellers. I wouldn't recommend it, though."

He chuckled and ran a hand through his hair, making my heart skip a beat. "No, I normally don't."

"I see. I just got lucky then." I smiled to show him that I was joking.

"Yes, well, I hope you'll forgive me and not hold it against me."

"Oh, it'll definitely be held against you," I teased. "But not in a bad way. More like...an inside joke."

He smiled. "That's a relief." He shuffled on his feet. "Not to be *that* banker, but I would appreciate it if you would think of me next time you need to refer anyone. I know I just got here, but I hope that we can have a good working relationship. You know, scratch my back, and I'll scratch yours?"

I returned his smile. "I'll keep you in mind."

He nodded, then turned back to his desk. Mark whistled lowly.

"What?" I asked.

"He couldn't take his eyes off you," he whispered with a conspiratorial grin.

I rolled my eyes. "I'm sure he's already introduced himself to everyone and made the same offer."

He let out a short laugh. "Nope. Introduced himself, yes. The offer, though? Not at all."

I waved him off. "He's just being nice after spilling his drink on me."

"Right. Keep telling yourself that."

In the Vault

ETHAN

AFTER MY RUN-IN WITH ASTRID IN THE BREAK ROOM, I found it difficult to concentrate. I knew I recognized her from somewhere, but for the life of me I couldn't place where from. It wasn't until I stepped into the back to get more coffee and check the dating app that it clicked. She had been on here. I had passed her by when I saw the photo of her drinking with her friends.

From our brief interaction, I could tell she was quiet, if not a little shy. I felt awful for spilling my coffee on her and was glad to see she'd had time to change before coming back to work.

I watched her from the corner of my eye after returning to my desk again. She seemed...happy. Carefree. She joked with her coworker, Mark, who was stationed next to her. Her laughter tinkled across the lobby, sounding full of joy. I couldn't explain my sudden fascination with her. I had written her off so quickly based on pictures from her profile, but perhaps I had been wrong about her. Regardless, she was a coworker, and dating someone from work was frowned upon. If things didn't work out and the pair weren't mature, it could result in an awkward workplace environment. Most times, when people started dating, the banks would transfer them, but since Central Bank was more of a credit union than a big-name bank, they didn't have anywhere to transfer them to.

I was thinking about it too much. She was off-limits as far as I was concerned. I returned my focus to my emails but found it hard to concentrate. Needing to distract myself, I decided I could walk along the teller line. Maybe even chat with some of the other tellers. Deciding that's what I would do, I wheeled my chair back and made my way to the teller line, making sure I started on the opposite side of Astrid.

The other tellers ignored me, but were cordial when I introduced myself. However, they were busy with their own conversations with each other, so I just stood silently behind them in case they needed anything. Part of my job was to assist with overrides and to get them more money if they needed it. Usually, at least one banker stayed behind the line for this reason, but the other bankers didn't seem too keen to do so here.

Part of me hoped Astrid would need help. I felt my body heat in response to just thinking about being in the cramped space of her teller station with her behind me. Feeling my blood beginning to pump to lower, more private regions, I quickly started thinking of other things. *After work, I need to stop by the store to get puppy food and a dish. I should also take Sophia to the animal shelter to find a puppy. I did promise her, after all, and she's been patiently waiting.*

"Hey, Ethan?" A delicate voice distracted me from my thoughts.

Looking down the line, I saw the source: Astrid. She had a customer in front of her, and she was facing me expectantly. I made my way over to her, making sure to think only of work, and nothing else. I smiled at the customer.

"Good afternoon. How can I help?" I asked.

Astrid lowered her voice, "I need an approval for this gentleman's withdrawal and to get into the vault."

I nodded once, then slipped into her station as she moved aside. The heat from her body caressed my side, trying to draw me into it. I turned my attention to her screen, making it my focus as I attempted to ignore my wayward thoughts. I glanced over the man's account, making sure everything was kosher with his finances. He had plenty in the account to cover the transaction, and these types of withdrawals were standard for him, so no warning signs there.

"Hi, Mr. Benson, how are you today?" I asked, making light conversation.

"Doing just great. Bout to start renovating our bathroom," he replied cordially.

"Oh wow! That's a big project. Are you trying to get the house ready to sell or just updating?"

"Just updating. The wife wants one of those fancy stand-up showers and a jacuzzi tub." Mr. Benson chuckled and shook his head. "First it was the kitchen, now it's this. I swear the projects never end."

I smiled. "No, they don't, but I'm sure she appreciates your hard work."

He nodded. "She does, she does." He winked at me. "Gotta keep the wife happy, am I right?"

I laughed. "Yes, sir." I approved the transaction, then locked Astrid's computer for her. "We will be right back, Mr. Benson."

"Of course! Take your time. I'm in no hurry."

Astrid followed me to the vault, and I tried to ignore the fact that we were going to be in close proximity until this transaction was over. Her scent of vanilla and cardamom was still stuck in my nose, making it hard to concentrate, and I had to redo the code to the vault.

"Forget it already?" she teased lightly.

45

I chuckled. "No. Just missed a number."

It clicked and swung open. I motioned for her to go first, then followed her in, immediately regretting the decision when her perfume enveloped me. Her yelp of surprise brought me back to my senses, and I reached out to grab her as she began to fall forward.

Her warm body collided with mine as I caught her, turning her around, and pulling her to me and to safety from whatever had tripped her. Her wide brown eyes met mine in surprise, a delicate blush forming on her cheeks. She was so close...

My hand was sprawled across her back as I lifted her back to standing. Her hand rested carefully on my chest. Her face was only a mere few inches from mine, so close I could just lean down and...

"Thank you," she whispered, tearing me from my thoughts.

"Of course," I whispered back.

I cleared my throat and stepped back, putting a safe distance between us. I glanced down to see that a safety deposit box had been left haphazardly on the floor. She made an annoyed noise as she knelt to pick it up and put it back in its place on the shelf.

"Some of the other tellers, I tell you," she muttered under her breath before walking further in towards where the hundreds were stacked.

I helped her count the money she needed, then followed her out, closing and locking the vault behind us. Then we took Mr. Benson to another room where I sat next to her and watched her count it out to him. I tried to ignore the fire that had ignited inside of me from our near-kiss in the vault. Tried to block out the memory of feeling her body flush against mine.

"Would you like an envelope, Mr. Benson?" she asked, her voice gentle.

"No, ma'am. I'll just slide them right here in my breast pocket," he said as he did precisely that. "Thank you both very much for your assistance. Now I'm off to the hardware store!"

I chuckled and stood along with him and Astrid. Holding out my hand, I said, "Good luck with your bathroom renovations, Mr. Benson. It's quite the undertaking!"

"Ah, I got nothin' better to do anyhow."

Astrid giggled. "Next up will probably be the living room."

"Ah, now, don't put any birdies into my wife's ear now!" Mr. Benson replied, laughter in his voice, as we followed him out of the room.

"I swear I won't," she replied, closing the door behind us and then returning to her station swiftly.

I followed leisurely behind, not wanting to tip her off to my eagerness to be close to her again. Though I should probably keep my distance, I found her drawing me in. I began to walk past her station when she turned to me.

"Thank you, Ethan, for, um, catching me so I didn't hurt myself," she commented.

I stopped and faced her. "Of course. Don't need any work injuries." I smiled, trying to play it off like it didn't impact me, even though it did.

I could see from the heat in her cheeks that it had affected her, too. Mark's gaze volleyed between us before he turned his attention forward. I knew from seeing them chatter already that he would probably ask her about it after I left.

"Yes, well, I appreciate it nonetheless. Now I only have a stubbed toe and not a broken arm or twisted ankle as well." She smiled softly.

I nodded, then moved to a more central spot on the teller line. I replayed the moment in my head. Her soft gasp. Her beautiful, wide eyes. The closeness and feel of her body against mine. The smell of her perfume, or body wash, or whatever it was that caused her to smell so delicious.

I glanced over to see that, sure enough, Mark was talking to her. Her eyes caught mine briefly, then she quickly looked away, a slight flush coming to her cheeks. I would definitely have to keep my distance. I didn't want another woman like my ex-wife. Not that I could definitively know that Astrid was like her, but I was also her coworker. That alone put her off limits.

I just needed to keep myself in check around her and shut down the attraction that had flared up in that vault.

After work, I drove to the after-school program that Sophia went to until I could pick her up. She practically bounced her way to the truck, rambling about her first day at her new school.

"And this girl named Beatrix said we could be the best of friends. She has blonde hair like me, but she has blue eyes. And Mrs. Scott said that I could sit next to her as long as we still paid attention and didn't distract each other. I also learned that Antarctica is where the penguins live. Did you know that, Daddy?" she asked.

"I did. Did you know that polar bears *don't* live there, though?" I returned as I opened her door.

She climbed inside. "She taught us that, too! She said penguins *also* live in Africa! Can you believe it?!"

I gasped. "Really? I thought they only liked the cold."

"Well, apparently, they also live there."

"That's so cool." I paused as I closed her door, then got into the driver's seat. "Hey, guess what?"

"What?"

"We are going to go to the animal shelter," I paused and watched her eyes light up, my heart warming at the sight, "right now!"

She squealed and bounced in her seat. "To get a puppy?!"

I nodded at her in the rearview mirror. "You'll have to make sure you find one you *really* like and will take care of."

"Oh, I will! I will be the bestest puppy taking carer there ever was."

"I know you will." I smiled at her.

"How was your day, Daddy?"

"It was good. Boring bank stuff, though."

"There were no thiefs?"

"Nope. Not today."

"Well, that's good. We don't like thiefs."

"No. No, we don't." I chuckled.

As I pulled into the shelter lot, I crouched down in front of her. "Now, remember. We can't take *all* of the puppies home. Only one. So find—"

"The one I really like," she parroted.

I smiled and nodded. Grabbing her hand, we walked into the shelter together and let the lady lead us to the puppies. There were two litters. One was a black lab mix, and the other looked like a husky. Both energetic breeds that would be great running partners for me when they got older.

Sophia decided she liked the huskies better and went into the pen. Puppies swarmed her, and her giggling seemed to make the room glow brighter. I smiled, loving the sound of her little laugh. One puppy in particular paid the most attention to her. It was a little female pup with bright blue eyes in a rouge mask. Her coloring was white and red in the classic husky coat.

"I like this one, Daddy," Sophia said as she picked the poor pup up around its front legs.

It reached up to lick and nip at her face, making her giggle.

"That's the one you want, then?" I asked.

She nodded. "Yup, she's the best one."

"Alright then! Let's take her out front and get you going," the attendant said as she hooked a leash onto the puppy and handed it to Sophia.

As I filled out the paperwork, I overheard Sophia already trying to train the puppy. I could hear the excitement in her voice, and I was glad I decided to do this today.

"What're you going to name her, Soph?" I asked.

"Hmm," she said, thinking. "I think I'll name her... Rosy."

"Rosy?"

"Yes, Rosy. Because she's red."

"That's a great name then."

I finished the paperwork, paid for her, then we drove to the pet store, taking Rosy in with us. We picked out a crate, dog bowls, puppy chow, pee pads, and some toys, then headed home. Sophia immediately started taking Rosy around the house, the sounds of the puppy's paws chasing after her making me smile. It would be good for her to have a little buddy. It would help ease her into this transition to a new home and a new school. Not that she seemed to be having a hard time, but I knew that sometimes kids kept their suffering to themselves.

That night, I had a dream about Astrid.

I had pulled her close to me, just like I had in the vault. Her body was flush against mine, and I gave in to the desire to kiss her. Her lips were soft and warm. She let out a breathless gasp as I kissed down her neck, pulling her tighter against my body. Her hands gripped my shirt as I placed kisses along her collarbone, drawing out a soft moan from her.

I awoke with a start, sitting up in bed as I fought to catch my breath. My heart hammered in my chest, and I looked down to see my hard-on tenting my blankets. I ran a hand through my hair as I flopped back onto my bed. This wasn't good. I couldn't be dreaming about her. I needed to keep my distance from her, not fantasize about her.

The memory of her soft moan played on repeat in my head, making it hard to fall asleep again. Did she actually sound like that, or was that just my brain thinking she did? I knew what her gasps sounded like. I could recall it from the small gasp that had escaped her in the vault.

Blood rushed to my cock again, and I groaned, pulling the pillow next to me on top of my head.

This wasn't helping.

I threw the pillow off me and stepped out of bed. Storming down to the kitchen, I heated some milk, then went to check on Sophia. She was sound asleep, her sleeping puppy cradled in her arms. I smiled and carefully shut her door so I wouldn't wake them. Then I climbed back into my own bed, gulped down the milk, and relaxed onto the pillows once again.

I hoped my brain would just let me sleep, without any dreams about a particular blonde teller.

Moving On

ASTRID

Mark
HAS SHE TOLD YOU ABOUT THE VAULT YET?!

Georgia
What happened to the vault?

Mark
Not what happened TO it, but what happened IN IT

Astrid
It was nothing…

Mark
Uh, excuse me, ma'am. It was NOT nothing!

Rose
What're you going on about?

Mark
The new banker almost kissed Ash in the vault!!!!

Astrid
He did not... He just saved me from falling, that's all

Daisy
Spill!

Astrid
I tripped on a safety deposit box someone had left out, and he caught me. He pulled me up to him to keep me from falling, that's all

Mark
And was sooo close to her! Their faces were inches apart

Rose
!!!!! Hot!

Astrid
Yes, that's true... But he wasn't going to KISS me

Mark
Sure. Keep telling yourself that

I SIGHED. THIS WAS RIDICULOUS. MARK WAS OVER-exaggerating it to our friends, and I rolled my eyes, but couldn't keep the smile from spreading across my face. It had taken everything to keep him calm during our workday. He had about squealed when I had informed him of what happened in the vault.

Thinking on it, my body warmed in response as my core clenched. It had been so hot... I couldn't lie to myself. The way he had gazed down at me, then at my lips, had been unmistakable. There was no way for it to have been my imagination. I had felt his attraction prodding into my stomach.

My cheeks flushed at the memory.

Fucking hell, it had been hot.

I wondered briefly if he would have kissed me if I hadn't broken the spell he had seemed to be under.

What was I thinking? I shook my head. He was a coworker. Yes, he was attractive, but I had promised myself not to fall for another coworker. It got too awkward when things didn't work out. *But what if things did work out?* I shook my head again. No. No thinking like that.

I unlocked my apartment door, and my phone chimed.

New Message from Theodore

Theodore? Who was that? Curious, I pulled up the message. It was from the dating app. A handsome face appeared on my screen. Theodore had brown hair, brown eyes, freckles, and an adorable smile. A few pictures showed him riding a Harley and welding something. *A welder? Interesting.*

Theodore
Howdy. How was your day?

I liked that he had skipped the usual "How are you" messages in favor of something that could be answered with actual meat.

Astrid
It was pretty good. Just work though.
Nothing overly exciting. What about you?

Theodore
It was good. Welded a few projects for
work, then relaxed the rest of the day.

Theodore
So, what do you like to do?

I started a small pot of rice while I thought about how to answer that. I hadn't really given it much thought. What *did* I like to do?

Astrid
Well, I like to go for walks in the park when the weather is nice. Otherwise, I'm content reading or watching a TV show.

Theodore
What's your favorite show?

Astrid
Right now, I would say Schitt's Creek. You?

Theodore
Same! I love that show. David cracks me up.

Astrid
He is so funny!

We chatted for hours after that about little things. It was a nice change of pace. He didn't rush into the meeting right away or focus only on small talk, either. He asked more profound questions, like what my life goals were and where I saw myself in the next few years. The conversation didn't stop until I was in bed, snuggled up with only my phone peeking out from the covers.

Astrid
Well, I need to head to bed as I have work tomorrow. It was really nice talking with you

> **Theodore**
> Same time tomorrow?

> **Astrid**
> Lol sure

> **Theodore**
> It's a date then 😊

I giggled then sighed happily. This was good. I could forget about Ethan and focus on Theodore instead. So long as he was actually a good guy, that is. *So much for not dating for a while*, I chided myself. Then again, who was I to hold myself back? I couldn't find Mr. Right if I weren't actively looking for him after all.

I giggled then sighed happily. This was good. I could forget about Ethan and focus on Theodore instead. So long as he was actually a good guy, that is. *So much for not dating for a while*, I chided myself. Then again, who was I to hold myself back? I couldn't find Mr. Right if I weren't actively looking for him after all.

Throughout the week, I did my best to avoid Ethan. It helped that he seemed to be doing the same. It irked Mark, however, who was adamant that we should be together, for whatever reason I couldn't conceive. I reminded him time and time again that I wasn't going to date someone with whom we worked. I had enough things to worry about without having to avoid men in the workplace.

Theodore and I continued to talk on the app over the next week. He was definitely taking his time to get to know me, and I appreciated that about him. The girls also thought it was sweet, and Mark begrudgingly agreed. We really seemed to click, and I couldn't wait for the weekend, as we had decided to go on a date together finally. The excitement continued to ramp up each passing day.

Friday finally arrived, and I was excited to get the day over with since I would be meeting Theodore tonight. I was so caught up in my head that I was caught off guard when Mark leaned over.

"Asher didn't show up to work today," he whispered, eyeing the banker's area.

I glanced over, and sure enough, his desk sat empty and vacant. I shrugged. "Not my problem."

He gave me a sarcastic look. "No, but it's concerning. He's *never* missed a day of work."

Now that I thought about it, he was right. Asher hadn't ever missed a day of work. I glanced at his desk again, wondering where he was. Regardless, though, it wasn't any of my business.

Later that day, the whispers began.

I returned from lunch break, and the eyes followed me. Feeling uncomfortable, I slipped into my station and tried to ignore them, unsure why they would suddenly be staring at me.

"Did you know?" Mark leaned over to whisper, his eyes wide.

I glanced up, a brow raising. "Know what?"

"That he was part of a gang."

I blinked and scrunched up my face. "Who? What?"

"Asher! Did you know he was part of some gang that apparently runs just about the whole city?"

I shook my head, eyes going wide. "No. Where on earth did you hear such a thing?"

"It's all over the news. Girl... He was shot in an alleyway when he tried to kidnap his ex-girlfriend and leave with her. The SWAT team showed up and killed him."

Shock rolled over me in waves, mixed with a tinge of grief. While I couldn't say I had truly loved Asher, I thought I had and had enjoyed our time together, and to hear this... It was beyond what I could have possibly thought possible. His lies went deeper than just stringing me along and cheating on Chloe. This was... I didn't even know how to process this. I sat down on my stool, unable to hold myself up.

"I had no idea," I whispered. Then I glanced back up at Mark, "Is that why everyone is looking at me funny?"

He nodded. "I'm so sorry, Ash."

"What for?"

"Well... That he's, you know...dead."

"I mean, it's awful, but I'm not heartbroken over it. I'm just in shock. I had no idea his lies ran so deep. What else was he hiding?"

Mark shrugged. "Only the police would know."

I nodded. Of course. I would never know.

But that was alright.

I took a deep breath to steady myself.

Asher was gone, and while I couldn't fathom what all he had done or what his ex-girlfriend was going through, part of me was glad I never had to see him again. As awful as that was. Did I wish death on him? Of course not. But it sure made working here a little easier.

Gone was the weight of his threat upon my shoulders.

Gone was the awkwardness of seeing him after everything had ended.

I could finally, once and for all, move on.

Later that night, I went home to change. I decided to wear something casual, since we were going to dinner and a movie. I pulled out jeans and a nice t-shirt. As I slipped them on, I thought about how nice it would be to dress like me for a change, without trying to impress. I smiled at myself in the mirror as I pulled my long locks into a ponytail, then tugged some baby hairs out along my hairline.

I locked the door behind me and then made my way downstairs. I had told Theodore I would meet him at the restaurant because I didn't want to share my location just yet. Brad had taught me not to do that. Things could go south, and the last thing I wanted was another man begging at my teller station or front door.

I pulled into the parking lot of Bob's Grill. It was a busy night, seeing as how it was Friday, and most likely a football game would be playing on virtually every screen inside. I didn't mind much. It was entertaining watching men yell at a screen as if the players could hear them. I walked inside and looked around. I didn't see any men hanging around waiting, so I pulled out my phone to message Theodore.

Astrid
Hey! Just arrived. Are you here?

Theodore
Pulling in now. Be right there!

"Hi, how many?" a waitress asked as she came up to the counter.

"Oh, it'll be two. My date just arrived and will be—" I started.

"Here I am," a man called out, rushing forward. "You beat me! I was hoping that if I left early enough, I would beat you here."

I took him in. He was taller than me, and his brown eyes drew me in. They sparkled with mischief and excitement. I smiled at him.

"No worries. I'm usually way early to everything," I told him.

"Duly noted," he replied.

"So, two?" the waitress asked again.

"Yes, yes. Two, please," Theodore answered.

He motioned me to go first as we followed the waitress to a table by the outer wall.

"Your server will be with you shortly," she said before placing down our menus and walking away.

"So, how was your day?" Theodore asked, his eyes taking me in.

"It was...Interesting," I replied, glancing at the menu. "How was yours?"

"Wait, backpedal. What do you mean by 'interesting'?"

I looked back up to see him leaning forward in interest, his eyes never having left my face. I flushed, not used to the attention. Well, I had Mark and the girls who would pay attention to me, but not someone like Theodore. It was refreshing, but also something I was unused to.

"Well, I learned that my ex, who I worked with, died today, and that he was part of a gang."

He blinked a few times. "Oh, wow. That's a bombshell to drop. You seem to be handling it okay."

I shrugged. "I'm sad for the guy, but I'm also...relieved that he's gone? I know that sounds horrible, I just don't know how else to put it."

He shook his head. "I don't think it's horrible. That's a perfectly human response, I would think. You must have had a nasty breakup, though."

"You could say that."

"Hey there, folks. I'm Marshall, and I'll be taking care of you tonight," a waiter greeted as he came up to our table. "Can I get you started with some drinks?"

"I'm okay with just water," I told him.

"Same, thank you," Theodore replied.

"Alright, making my job easy tonight!" Marshall chuckled. "Are you ready to order?"

Theodore looked to me with a raised brow, making my stomach do flip-flops. "I am if you are."

"Yeah, I am," I replied quietly. "Can I get the southwestern salad, please?"

"You got it," Marshall said. "And for you, sir?"

"The western burger, please, thanks," Theodore replied, handing over our menus.

"Coming right up!"

"You must come here often. You didn't even look at the menu," I commented.

His lips quirked in a smirk. "Every Friday night."

"For football?"

"No. I just like their food. I couldn't care less about football."

"Really? A man who doesn't like to yell at the TV screen when someone doesn't make the right pass or the referee makes a bad call?" I smirked at him, not believing him for a second.

"Really. I prefer to watch things actually worth my time."

"Ah, yes. Like Schitt's Creek. Because that is definitely worthy of spending time on."

He chuckled. "When you are tired and trying to relax, yes."

"Okay, I'll give you that."

There was a brief lull in our conversation before he said, "You're a lot more beautiful than I thought. Your pictures don't do you justice."

My heart stopped as a blush crept onto my cheeks, and I suddenly felt hot. "Oh, well, thank you."

He grinned. "You're very welcome."

Conversation flowed easily from there, and I found myself

falling for him. He was so easy to be around, just like Brad had been. The thought made me put up my guard. I tried to ignore it, but warning bells pealed in my mind regardless.

After dinner, we met at the movies. He paid for our tickets and then led us to the theater, a hand on my lower back to guide me. The heat from his hand raced along my spine and to my very core, pooling there. As the movie began, he put an arm around my shoulders, and I leaned in, all thoughts and warnings that had been playing in my mind completely forgotten.

During the movie, his thumb absentmindedly stroked along my arm. It was intoxicating and distracting, so much so that I could hardly remember most of what the movie was about by the time it had finished. After the movie, he walked me to my car.

"I had a really great time tonight, Astrid," he confessed, standing so close to me that I could feel his body heat coming off of him in waves.

"I did, too," I replied, looking up into his brown eyes.

His gaze drifted down to my lips before returning to my eyes. Then he whispered, "I would really like to kiss you."

My breath hitched. "So kiss me then."

He stepped forward, placing his hands on either side of me against my car, and leaned forward. My heart hammered in my chest as our lips met. It was soft, gentle, and careful. He stepped forward again, our bodies pressing against each other as my backside met the car door. I couldn't move, but I didn't want to. One of his hands slipped behind the nape of my neck, cupping the back of my head and deepening our kiss. I moaned softly as I felt him harden, his thick length pushing against my stomach and taunting me.

He pulled away, both of us breathless. "Wow," he finally said.

I nodded, completely at a loss for words.

"Do you want to come back to my hotel room?"

"Hotel room?"

"Yeah, I'm staying in a hotel while I'm on this job. I normally live over in Grandview, but my job can be 'come here and now' sometimes."

"Oh, that's right. I remember you saying that."

He pulled me in for another kiss, and I melted into it. Then he rested his forehead on mine. "Please?"

"I-I don't know..."

"I want to worship your body."

Well, fuck. When he put it like that... "Okay."

"Okay?" He grinned, pulling back slightly.

"Okay. Alright. I'll come over. But just this once."

His grin widened even further as he stepped back. "Good. I'll text you the address."

I really hoped I was making the right decision. I texted the group chat to let them know the night's newest development, then waited for him to text the address.

Theodore
Brantley Suites, room 316

Oh. He was staying in the fanciest hotel in town. Either his job really spoiled their employees, or he made a *lot* of money. I headed that way, my insides quivering with anticipation. As I parked, I took a deep breath, willing myself to stay calm. Then I made my way up to his room and knocked on the door. It swung open immediately, and he pulled me inside, devouring my mouth with a new energy. Like my being here had unleashed something inside of him.

I moaned as he nipped my jawline, finding that sweet spot behind my ear. I could feel myself already dripping wet as he slid a hand under my shirt and around to my back to unclasp my bra. With expert ease, it was undone in a flash, then his hand found my breast, pinching and kneading my nipple and sending bolts of lightning through my body. I gasped, his mouth swallowing the sound.

I grabbed onto his shirt for dear life, feeling like I was being swept away with the voracity with which he was exploring my body. He lifted my shirt over my head, then peeled off my bra and cast them aside, his mouth trailing hot kisses down my chest. I moaned and grabbed onto his hair, hoping to have some stability. He pulled away, and I whined before I noticed him eyeing me hungrily.

"You are so fucking beautiful," he growled before sweeping me off my feet and carrying me to the bedroom.

He lay me down gently on the bed, then trailed kisses down my stomach while his hands ran down along my sides, tracing my curves. I sighed, enjoying the feeling of my body being adored for once. His fingers hooked into my pants, and he looked up at me, a begging question in his eyes. I bit my lip and nodded. He pulled them down slowly, trailing kisses down my hips to my thighs. He withdrew to pull them off completely, then knelt in front of me.

"I can see your wetness through your thong," he murmured as he trailed a finger along its hem.

I whimpered and fought not to squirm.

He slipped a finger beneath them, caressing the edges of me. I couldn't help the squirm. I needed more. Instead, he wrapped one of his arms around my waist, effectively locking me in place. He continued to caress me, slowly and deliberately, working his way up to my clit. It was maddening, but as soon as he touched my sensitive bud, my eyes rolled back as I gasped. He circled it, teasing it ever so slowly. And just as I was about to peak, his hand vanished. I nearly wept at the denial.

"Oh, don't you worry. I'm not finished with you yet," he growled as he slid my thong down and tossed it aside. "I'm just getting started."

Then his tongue lapped at me, and I lost it. My back arched off the bed, my hands gripping the sheets tightly as if they could deliver me from this delicious torture that I both wanted to crest, but also never wanted to end. He sucked on me, and it sent chills through my body that built me higher and higher. I could feel my orgasm coming, and I knew it would hit me hard like a supernova.

Just as I was about to tip over the edge, he slipped a finger inside me, curling it just so. I came in a wave of stars cascading around me, screaming out in pleasure as I rode wave after wave of it. I had never had such an intense orgasm before, and it left me breathless in its wake. Sweat was beading upon my brow, and my body shivered in response to the mind-blowing satisfaction that had just detonated in my core.

"Damn, that was hot," Theodore whispered as he appeared above me.

Sometime between delivering the best orgasm of my life and climbing atop me, he had gotten undressed. I barely had a moment to process it before I felt his cock nudging at my entrance. He pushed in slowly, the stretch of him leaving me breathless.

"Oh fuck, you feel so good."

I nodded, unable to speak. I inhaled sharply as he suddenly drove forward, driving himself in to the fullest. I could feel every delicious inch of him within me, and I craved more. He pulled back slowly, then drove forward again, fast and hard. I moaned, grabbing onto him for dear life. He did it again, and I cried out in both pain and pleasure. It felt so good.

"You like that?"

"Yes. Oh, fuck, yes," I moaned.

He continued at the same pace before it became erratic, building us both up. I could feel my core clenching and pulsating with every thrust. I found my release just as he slammed in with a groan, finding his own inside me. We panted, both breathless and covered in sweat. He chuckled and rested his forehead against mine.

"Well, damn. That was... More than I had anticipated to happen this evening," he told me.

I giggled. "Yeah. Same."

He rolled off of me and pulled me into him. "Totally worth it."

I closed my eyes and rested my head on his chest. "Completely."

Exhaustion took hold of my body and swept me away, the sound of his breathing lulling me to sleep.

Just Be Me

ASTRID

I WAS TOO HOT, AND SOMETHING WAS BUZZING. I opened my eyes, memories of last night coming back to me in a flood. Theodore's arm was draped over my waist, our legs intertwined. That explained how hot I was. I peered around the room, trying not to disrupt him, when I spied the phone on the bedside table. Thinking it was mine, I reached for it.

It wasn't.

It was Theodore's.

And a smiling woman's picture with the name "Monica" was calling him.

Beneath that?

The title - "Wifey".

What.

The.

Actual.

Fuck.

I placed the phone back on the table and pretended I hadn't seen it, but the questions were going wild in my mind. Who was Monica? Was he married? Certainly not. He couldn't be. I hadn't seen a ring on his finger, nor a tan line.

Nothing screamed that he was *married*. I had it wrong. It had to be a joke. There had to be an explanation for this.

"Mm, good morning, beautiful," he said as he pulled me in tighter and nuzzled against my neck.

"Morning. I, uh, I need to pee," I said, thinking of a reasonable excuse to get out of his arms and text the group.

I needed their input.

He pulled his arm off of me and grinned at me. "Don't be too long."

I gave him a half-hearted smile before walking to the restroom. It took everything in me to appear normal and not dash away from him. As soon as I closed the door behind me, I pulled out my phone.

> **Astrid**
> SOS!

> **Georgia**
> What's up?

> **Mark**
> Everything okay?

> **Astrid**
> His phone woke me up when someone tried calling him. I thought it was mine, so I looked at it. Someone named Monica was calling him, and under her name was her nickname "Wifey". What do I do?? Am I freaking out over nothing?

It took them a few moments to respond.

"Everything okay in there?" Theodore called.

"Yeah, everything's fine. I'll be out in just a second," I called back, panicking internally.

Mark
ABORT

Rose
I agree. Abort Mission Theodore. Get out of there fast

I nodded. Flushing the toilet, I left the bathroom and pretended to hold my stomach.

"Hey, I'm not feeling so great. I think I'm going to head home," I lied.

"Oh, shoot. Okay," he replied, jumping out of bed to walk me to the door. "I hope you start feeling better. Do you need anything? I can go to the store and grab some soup or something and bring it to you."

I waved him off. "No, no. That's alright. Thank you, though."

"Okay, well, text me when you can."

He pecked me on the cheek, then I made a mad dash to my car to get the heck out of there.

As soon as I parked outside my apartment, I dropped my head onto the steering wheel. What was it about me that attracted these losers? Did I scream "side piece" or something? Tears flooded my vision. I was tired of this. Tired of being strung along or lied to. Why can't men just be honest about their relationship status? My phone dinged.

Theodore
I think I know why you left, and I wanted to tell you that it's not what you think. Monica is my work wife. It's kind of a running joke, and I should have told you before this happened.

Astrid
Then why was she calling at 7 in the morning?

Theodore
They needed me at work. I'm so sorry.
Please believe me…

Astrid
I honestly don't know…

I really didn't. He might have been telling the truth, but there was also that nagging sense that he wasn't. I just couldn't get past it. Something was off. He was too nice, too concerned, too…playing the part. That, and he was staying in a hotel. When he supposedly only lived in the next town over, which was only thirty minutes from here. It just didn't add up.

Astrid
It could be that you are being truthful, but I can't take that chance. If you are, you are a very nice guy, and I'm sure there is someone out there for you. But that someone isn't me.

Theodore
I understand, and I'm so sorry again. I wish you believed me, but I can see that there is some broken trust there. One day, I hope you give a guy a chance.

I dropped my head back on the headrest. He had said it so..maturely, yet it also made me feel guilty—part of what he said was right. There definitely was broken trust when it came to men and their relationship status. However, I knew I wouldn't allow myself ever to be a side piece again.

One day, I hoped I could meet a guy who wasn't complicated or in a relationship. One that would actually be good for me.

But right now, I think I want it just to be me.

I deleted the dating app later that day and decided I would

take a break from all things men. They were nothing but liars, anyway. Maybe I'd get a cat. At least they didn't lie to you.

Later that day, I decided I would indeed get a cat and made an appointment at the local shelter. I'd spent most of the day getting everything in my apartment set up so that it would be ready to go when I brought my new fur-buddy home, then perused the ads on the shelter's website. There were a few cats I had in mind that sounded like the perfect addition to my lonely lifestyle.

One was a black tomcat. His "About Me" said he was a "lover boy" who preferred women to men. That would be perfect, but I also wondered if he might be too clingy. Another was a sweet calico girl. She was said to be playful and loved to snuggle, but also liked to have her space. Seeing as I worked, she might be better. Then there were the kittens, of course. Darling little things! There were five of them at the shelter right now. My only hesitancy about getting a kitten was that they were a lot of work and tended to need more attention than I could provide.

I'd also browsed the more senior cats. People tended to gravitate towards kittens or middle-aged cats, while leaving the older cats behind. I understood. People didn't want to love something so sincerely only for it to pass on a few months or years later, especially if they had kids. It hurt deeply to lose a pet. I'd had a few growing up and could still remember the pain of it as if it had happened yesterday. However much I wanted to help the senior cats, I didn't think it would be wise for me to take that on. Some had health issues, and vet bills could get expensive. So I decided I would check out the two adult cats that had caught my attention. I would also ask the shelter for any recommendations.

After I was satisfied that my apartment was ready, I drove to the shelter and took a deep breath as I pulled into the parking lot. Excitement quickly replaced the thoughts whirring in my head as I walked inside. Dogs barked in the distance, the sound jarring but also sad. I felt bad that they had to be locked away, awaiting a loving family to take them home. As I approached the main desk, a lady looked up.

"Hello. How can I help you?" she asked.

"Hi, I made an appointment to take a look at some of your cats," I told her.

"Astrid Hart?"

"Yes, ma'am."

She smiled. "Perfect. Follow me."

I followed her to a room to the right of her desk, quiet enveloping us as the door whooshed closed. They must have installed a soundproofing system to help the cats stay calm and not be bothered by the dogs' barking.

"So, what exactly are you looking for?" the woman asked, slightly turning as she unlocked another door.

Rows of smaller cages stacked upon one another were behind the door. Some were empty while others held the cats that had been on their website.

"Well, I work full-time, so I need a cat that will be alright on its own when I'm not there," I told her, peering into a kennel where an orange cat hid in the back. "But I also want one that's loving. I live alone, so I'd like someone to greet me, if you know what I mean?"

She chuckled. "I do. Lacey might be a good fit for you then."

She motioned to a kennel where the calico I had seen

online was rubbing against the bars. I smiled as I walked forward and rubbed her through the metal slats. The cat purred loudly and rubbed her face against my hand, her yellow eyes peering back at me in slits.

"I can take her out, and we can go to the visitation room, if you'd like," the woman suggested.

"That would be great, thank you."

She nodded and unlocked the cage. Lacey meowed at her as she reached in to lift her out. I followed her to another room that contained a couch and cat toys. I spent a few minutes letting Lacey roam, but she preferred to rub against our legs and climb onto our laps.

"And she will be alright on her own? She's not too clingy or dependent?" I asked as I stroked her face gently.

"Yes, she is sweet, but she also likes to be left alone after a while."

Just as she said this, Lacey jumped off my lap and began roaming around the room, completely ignoring us. I smiled.

"Perfect, I'll take her," I said.

"Great. Let me get her into a carrier while you fill out some paperwork. Do you have everything at home already for her?"

I nodded. "I do. I got everything set up last night, right down to the litter box. I didn't get any food yet aside from wet food since I didn't know what you feed her here."

She picked Lacey up and began carrying her back to the cages. "Oh, good. We feed them the scientific diet brand. You can grab a bag while you are here, but they also sell them at most vet clinics." She handed me a clipboard once we got to the desk. "Here. Fill this out, and we will be right back."

I nodded and busied myself with the form. It was pretty basic—name, address, phone number, and other general information, along with the cat's information. I decided I'd keep her name. It was cute and fitting. The woman came back with a white cardboard animal carrier just as I finished.

"She's already spayed and had her rabies vaccine last month. It's good for a year, so make sure you make her an appointment next year to get it renewed," she told me as she placed Lacey gently down beside me, then went back around the counter and typed in the information on the computer. "The cat adoption fee is $50."

I nodded and pulled out my card. A few minutes later, I was on my way home with Lacey in tow. She stayed quiet the whole ride, which was surprising. I had expected her to meow up a storm once we got moving. As soon as I got home, I crouched on the floor and opened the box. She peered out hesitantly before hopping out and looking around.

The research online said most cats are skittish for the first few weeks in a new environment, but her tail stood straight as she looked around. She began to walk around my small apartment, finding her litter box and food without a problem. I breathed a quiet sigh of relief. At least, I hoped she would be alright. I tsked her and she came running over, rubbing her head against my hand. I smiled down at her as I wrapped her new collar around her, the bell chiming softly.

"Welcome home, Lacey," I told her.

I walked back to my bedroom and heard her following behind me, her little bell tinkling. I chuckled as I watched her roam around my room while I got changed into a pair of yoga pants and a comfy sweatshirt. She rubbed against my legs before venturing off again. Following her to the living area, I went to the kitchen to make dinner.

A little later, she came up to me to rub her head against my legs, purr loudly, then walk off again. I watched her go to the window, curious what she was doing. She paused before jumping up to the top of her cat tree, sitting down, and looking outside, her head moving back and forth as she watched whatever held her attention. Her orange-and-black mottled tail swished back and forth. I grinned, knowing I had made the right choice.

False Promises

ETHAN

It was hard keeping my distance from Astrid, especially given that my mind liked to torture me with dreams of her virtually every night. I didn't know why. I kept telling myself she was off-limits. So why was I drawn to her?

I rubbed a hand down my face after another night of fighting off my dreams of her. Thank goodness it was the weekend. Maybe it would do me some good, and it would make my brain fixate on something else to torture me with. Like, I don't know, bank accounts gone wrong, or a swimsuit model. Anything and anyone but Astrid.

Though a part of me also enjoyed the dreams. Perhaps that was why I was so addicted to them subconsciously. Did she moan and whimper the way she did in my dream? Was her body as curvy as I imagined? Her nipples as perky, her pussy as...

FUCK.

I was *so* fucked.

I forced myself out of bed and into the shower—no more. I *had* to stop thinking like this. She was a coworker, and I would have to see her every day. I could not spend my hours away from her imagining what she would sound like, what her skin would feel like, how she would look under me...

NO.

Dammit.

I splashed my face with cold water.

My phone vibrating caught my attention, and I glanced at it before frowning. *Great. What does she want now? More money?*

Helena
Hey. I would like to know if we can meet today to talk.

Ethan
What is there to talk about, Helena?

Helena
I want to see Sophia...

Ethan
I don't think that's a good idea.

Helena
I really would like to start being a better mom and maybe even try us again...
Please, Ethan

I sighed, my heart squeezing painfully. I didn't know whether to trust her.

Helena
I've changed. I started talking to a therapist.

Ethan
We can meet for lunch, but I'm not bringing Sophia. You've hurt her enough, and I don't want to get her hopes up.

Helena
I'm her mother

Ethan
And you abandoned her

I hated cutting low like that, but I couldn't just let her walk back into Sophia's life whenever she felt like it. Sophia deserved better than that. She didn't need her mother to come around only when she felt like being a mom, then walk out again when it became too much of a demand. As much as I would love for Sophia to have a mother, I couldn't justify taking the chance that Helena had possibly changed. I needed to protect Sophia's heart and see if this change was permanent, or just because Helena had fallen on hard times again.

Ethan
Hey Leora. I know it's last-minute, but could you take Sophia this afternoon? Helena wants to meet up to talk about something.

Leora
Of course I can. I hope things go well.

Ethan
Thank you so much.

The plans made, I got ready for the day, my mind effectively distracted and now stressed about meeting with my ex-wife. I really didn't know what she could even say to prove she had changed. I wasn't one to hold a grudge or become calloused, but after how many months of trying to go to a counselor and work on the marriage, I didn't know how much more I could take.

Later that day, I dropped Sophia off, who happily ran off to play with Leora's son, Michael. Then I drove to the park where I said I would meet Helena. As I pulled into the parking lot, my gut twisted in apprehension when I saw her car. I parked next to her, and she got out, waiting for me with her arms wrapped around herself. She looked unsure, uneasy, cautious. I couldn't blame her. I felt the same.

"Thank you for meeting me, Ethan," she whispered as I approached.

I nodded once.

She looked away, taking a deep breath. "I wanted to apologize." Her eyes met mine again, begging me to listen. "I was an awful wife to you and a horrible mother to Sophia. I left when you needed me the most."

I bristled. That was just the tip of the iceberg. I tried not to react. She moved toward me, reaching out as if to caress my arm, but I pulled away. What game was she trying to play? I took in her appearance. She looked fragile. Almost sickly. Her cheeks looked flushed, and dark circles were under her eyes, a sure sign she had been drinking just the night before. I was surprised her hands weren't swollen, but maybe she hadn't drunk nearly as much as she had before our divorce. Back then, she would get puffy in her cheeks and hands from the fluid retention. Her weight would fluctuate between sickly thin and a few pounds overweight, mostly from either puking it all up or overeating to combat the alcohol. From all appearances, she just looked...stressed.

"Why are you here, Helena?" I asked.

"I told you, I want to see Sophia. I know I can't ask you to forgive me. I know you won't—"

"Oh, I forgave you long ago."

She looked relieved, and a smile appeared on her face.

"But that doesn't mean that I will let you break our daughter's heart. Again."

Her face fell. "I've changed, Ethan."

My eyes narrowed. "Have you? When's the last time you drank?"

Her face flushed.

"That's what I thought."

I started to walk back to my truck. This wasn't worth my time or effort.

"Ethan, please!" she called out, her voice pleading with me.

I whirled around and stormed back to her. "Why are you here?"

Her feet shuffled. "I-I need help."

"Help. Of course. You only come around when you *need* something. What about when I needed you as a wife? What about when Sophia needed her mother? Where were you then? Partying. Drinking. Sleeping around with who knows who." I shook my head. "If you need help, you came to the wrong place."

Tears glistened in her eyes. "I just want to see my little girl."

"No."

"Why? Why won't you let me see her?!"

"Because you left," I yelled, drawing the attention of people walking nearby. I took a deep breath. "Because you *left*. She was only five, Helena. And you left her. You left *us*. You abandoned our dream of living as a happy, loving family for the bottom of a bottle, and you didn't look back. You chose who to give your loyalty to. You chose what you would make a priority in your life. And it wasn't us."

She sniffled. "I want to try. I *am* trying."

I snorted. "Right. I've heard that one before."

"I started going to AA meetings. I relapsed last night for the first time in two months. I really am trying, Ethan. Please, just give me a chance."

I shook my head. "I can't. I can't risk you breaking her

heart again. She deserves so much more than that. She is finally settling into our new home and making—"

"New home? You sold the house?"

I glared at her. "Why would I have stayed somewhere that the memories were kept alive? It was hurting both of us."

"Where did you move to?"

I shook my head. I couldn't tell her. The last thing I needed was her tracking us down and showing up on our doorstep uninvited.

"Why can't you tell me?"

"Because it doesn't concern you."

She paused for a moment before quietly asking, "Did you meet with me just to tear me down?"

"No, Helena. I came to say goodbye."

"Goodbye?"

"Helena," I started, running a hand through my hair as I looked away from her. "You abandoned us. You made your choice. Now it's time you live with it. Do not call me again. Do not text me. *If* you are truly making a change, which I hope for your sake that you are, then you will be doing it without us in the picture. It's time we all let it go and move on." I took a deep breath. "Sophia is happy. *I* am happy. You need to find happiness, too."

"Ethan, I—"

I shook my head and walked away. It didn't matter what she said. I had said what I needed to, and she would have to live with her decision for the rest of her life. I could tell by looking at her that she still wasn't well. I hoped she would seek professional help if she weren't already, and that she would get the help she needed. But I didn't have to wait and watch for it to happen.

Maybe, once upon a time, I would have given her another chance. But today, I had made my decision. Today, she had solidified what I needed to know. She was only here because she had hit a low point. She had most likely run out of money. In which case, she would end up at her parents' house, because they still enabled her, and she would either find herself help or the bottle again. Either way, I didn't want to be a part of the cycle anymore, and Sophia didn't need to be a part of it either.

On my way home, I decided I would treat Sophia. At least it would distract me from the events of the day, and I could relax while also spending some quality time with her. I stopped at the store to grab ice cream, pizza, and a face mask, because she loved the darn things. I also picked out some new nail polish on a last-minute decision to paint her nails. She had been asking me for a while to do them, even though I hated it, so it was time I gave in. Then I headed to Leora's.

"How'd it go?" Leora asked in a whisper.

I sighed. "She looked rough. Sick. She said she's been going to AA and seeing a therapist, but she's said that how many times now?" I shook my head. "She begged to see Sophia."

She gave me a sympathetic smile and patted me on the shoulder. "I know it's hard, but you're doing the right thing. Sophia doesn't need anymore heartache. It's bad enough that her mom left her. She will carry that with her for the rest of her life."

"I know." I winced. "I just hope she doesn't blame herself. I've done my best to—"

"And you're doing a great job. She probably will still struggle with it. A lot of kids in this type of situation do. But she will pull out of it."

I nodded and made sure to put on a smile as I heard running feet coming down the hall.

"Daddy!" Sophia squealed as she barreled into me.

I bent down to pick her up and give her a tight hug. "Hey, kiddo. Ready to go home?"

"Yeah. I need to check on Rosy."

I chuckled. "Yes, we do. She probably has to go outside by now." I turned to Leora. "Thanks again."

"Any time. Bye, Sophia!"

"Bye," Sophia called, waving over my shoulder as I walked her to the truck.

"Did you have a good time?" I asked.

"Of course I did! Michael got this new game on his Play-Station called Minecraft. It's really cool. You can build homes and farm and stuff."

"Oh, yeah?"

"Yeah! He said they also have it on iPad. Can I get it?"

"We'll see, sweetie."

She hopped into the back of my truck as I held the door open, then squealed when she saw the bags on the backseat. "You got ice cream?!"

"I got more than just that. I thought we could have a daddy-daughter date night."

"Oh, yay! What else did you get?"

"You'll have to wait and see."

"Okay!"

She continued to talk a mile a minute about Minecraft and all the things you could do on our drive home. By the time we arrived, I knew a decent amount about the game. It sounded interesting, and I could see why she had enjoyed it so much. Rosy yipped and barked as we came in the door.

"I'm coming, Rosy!" Sophia called out as she raced to the kenneled pup and let her outside.

"I'll get the pizza going. Why don't you play outside while it cooks?" I called after her.

"Okay!"

Her peals of laughter came through the screen door as I preheated the oven. Watching her run around with the puppy in the backyard, I wondered whether I had truly made the right decision. What if Helena was telling the truth and she actually could become an active part of Sophia's life? But what if she relapsed again, only to leave Sophia worse off and with more questions? Self-doubts and what-ifs plagued my mind. I sighed, trying to silence them. There was no use in wallowing in them. I could only move forward from here.

Later that night, Sophia and I snuggled up on the couch to watch her favorite Disney princess movie for the five-hundredth time. Her nails were painted a vibrant pink, and her face was freshly cleaned. Rosy lay on Sophia's legs, with her head on her lap. I absentmindedly pet the dog every once in a while, and Sophia's head began to droop before too long.

I smiled, looking down at her sleeping peacefully with her head resting against my side. Her long lashes rested upon her childish cheeks. Despite our circumstances, I was thankful I had her in my life. Since the day she was born, my life had been brighter and full of so much more meaning.

I picked her up carefully and carried her to her room, Rosy trudging along behind me. Then I tucked her in, Rosy hopping up to rest at her feet, and kissed her on the forehead.

"Goodnight, Sophia. I love you to the moon and back," I whispered, then turned into bed myself.

Night Out

ASTRID

SUNDAY EVENING, THE GALS, MARK, AND I HAD agreed to get together at Midnight Society to gossip and catch up. It had been a couple of weeks since we'd been able to get together, and I was anxious to see them. I chose a cute blue dress with strappy heels, fixed up my hair, and did my makeup before checking on Lacey. She was sound asleep on her cat tree, soaking up the last rays of sunshine. I gave her a quick pet, her quiet meow of protest at being disturbed making me chuckle.

It amazed me how well she had settled in. She had spent most of the rest of yesterday occasionally roaming, but mostly on her cat tree, car and people watching. That night, she had slept at my feet, not seeming to want me out of her sight. She wasn't clingy, but she was definitely showing signs that she was already comfortable and attached to me, in her own way. I kissed her little head.

"Bye, Lacey, I'll be back later tonight," I told her. "Behave while I'm away!"

She didn't even budge. I chuckled, then grabbed my purse and coat before heading to Midnight Society. The club wasn't too far from home, so I decided to walk. The night air would be good, especially afterward. Not that I ever liked getting anything more than a slight buzz, but I loved the night air, and it helped me cool off. I always got hot in the club because there were so many people there, especially on a weekend night.

Tonight was no different.

Motorcycles and other vehicles filled the parking lot. *Hopefully, they already got a table*, I thought briefly before pushing open the dark glass doors. I paused just inside, letting the familiar bass beats thump through me while I looked for my friends. I was on my second sweep over the tables when I saw Rose standing and waving her arms above her head. I grinned and maneuvered my way over.

"Hey! Glad you made it," she yelled over the bass as I slipped in beside Daisy.

"Me too! I need this," I confessed.

Daisy turned toward me. "Spill!"

I rolled my eyes. "He claimed it was a 'work wife'."

"Oh, honey," Georgia tutted in her Southern accent. "You have been having some shit luck here lately. I'm so sorry."

I shrugged. "I decided to take a break. I got a cat!"

Rose screwed up her face, while her twin sister, Daisy, got excited.

"A cat?! What kind?" Daisy asked.

"She's a calico. Her name is Lacey," I told her.

"Aw! I want to come meet her!"

"Of course you do," Rose commented, rolling her eyes.

"Cats are great! They keep the mice away at the barn," Georgia said. "And some of them are so cuddly."

Rose gave her a sarcastic look. "Seriously? Cats are assholes."

"Lacey is super sweet," I told her.

"For now, just watch, once she gets comfortable, she'll

start attacking you for no reason and knocking your shit onto the floor."

I laughed and shook my head. Then I looked around, noticing a key person was missing from our group. "Where's Mark?"

"Getting drinks," Georgia answered. "There's been a long line."

"I'll go see if he needs help."

The girls nodded, and I slipped out before weaving my way through the crowd to get to the bar. As I got closer, I saw a familiar dark, tall, handsome man with his arm around a dark-haired beauty. He turned and saw me, eyes going wide. The woman turned, wondering what had caught his attention. I scoffed. Theodore was here with his "work wife" Monica. Go figure. Monica raised a brow and turned to Theodore, saying something in his ear. He quickly looked away from me, shaking his head in response to whatever it was that she had said.

I was about to turn away when I saw Mark a few feet away from them. So instead, I lifted my head and strutted past them. Pretending as if they didn't exist and I hadn't seen them. Just as I was passing by, however, a hand snagged my arm and pulled me back. I turned to see who it was and came face to face with none other than Monica.

"Can I talk to you for a minute?" she asked.

I looked around us. Theodore had disappeared. I hesitated.

"Please? Woman to woman?" she begged.

A million questions whirled in my mind. What did she want? What had she said to Theodore? Where the hell did he go? And most importantly, why did she want to talk to me? I faced her head-on and nodded, motioning for her to speak.

"I just want to know why Teddy recognized you," she

yelled over the bass. "I've had a hunch he's been cheating on me since taking on this job."

Oh, great. "Uh, I think this is a conversation you should have with him," I replied and tried to walk away.

Her hand squeezed painfully on my arm, her nails digging in. I hissed and turned back to face her.

"Please. I just need to know if I need to break off our engagement," she pleaded.

I could see the fear in her eyes. She hadn't accused me of anything. In fact, she seemed to know the answer already, but just needed a confirmation. I sighed heavily, my guard dropping. She noticed it immediately, tears filling her eyes as she nodded.

"I figured," she said. "Thank you. I'm sorry he led you on."

Then she walked away.

"What was that about?" Mark asked as he came up beside me with a tray of drinks that he was barely holding onto.

I took a couple of drinks off the tray. "Tell you at the table."

He nodded and followed after me, now managing the tray a lot easier since it wasn't completely loaded with drinks. I recognized the ones in my hand immediately: a Sea Siren for Daisy and a Long Island Tea for Georgia. I distributed them once I got to the table, then sat back down, Mark sliding in behind me.

"*Now* will you tell me what that lady was clawing onto you for?" he asked, turning toward me.

The girls perked right up, eyes going wide as they turned to me with expectation.

"That was Monica," I said bluntly.

A collective gasp went around the table.

"The 'wifey'?" Mark finally asked.

I nodded. "She was asking if she needed to break off the

engagement with Theodore. I guess she had suspected him of cheating on her while on this project."

"Oh," Daisy said. "Oh, my."

"Was she mad at you?" Mark asked.

I shook my head. "No. She wasn't upset with me at all. In fact, she even apologized *to me*."

Incredulous looks came across their faces.

"That's crazy," Rose shook her head.

"Glad you ran for the hills on that one," Georgia added.

"Me too," I replied.

"Now you can finally turn your attention to that new banker," Mark teased as he nudged me.

I rolled my eyes. "No. I'm done dating for a while. It's going to be just me and Lacey. Besides, I told you: no. Coworkers. It was bad enough with Asher."

"Speaking of..." Rose began.

"I don't want to talk about it."

She raised her hands.

"Well, on the topic of guys..." Rose looked down at her drink, suddenly shy. "There's a wonderful man who keeps coming into the coffee shop."

"Oohhhh," the rest of us said in unison, causing a bout of laughs to go around the table.

"Do tell," Mark said, leaning forward.

"Well, he rides a motorcycle," she started.

"And?" I prodded.

"He's tall. Dark. Handsome."

"Oh, so you're reading another romance novel," Mark joked.

Chuckles followed.

Rose rolled her eyes. "He wears a brown leather jacket and has some tattoos."

"So, what's his name?" Georgia asked as she sipped her tea.

"That's the thing. He gives a different name each time."

"That's a little…"

"Red flag!" Mark declared.

"Or maybe he's just shy," Daisy suggested. "Maybe he wants to be a mystery."

I saw her sigh. She was clearly attracted to the guy, but I wasn't the right one to give my opinions right now. Clearly, I hadn't recognized red flags until now, and I was working through some trust issues in the men's department. So I kept my mouth shut, even though I agreed with both Daisy and Mark. Either the guy was keeping secrets or just being coy. Time would tell.

"So, tell us about this banker that you keep pushing Astrid toward," Georgia brought me out of my thoughts.

"Well, he's single, that's the most important thing," Mark said with flair, looking pointedly in my direction.

I rolled my eyes and pretended to ignore him. What did he know that I didn't?

"He drives a truck that's got lots of bells and whistles. He's super nice, but also quiet. Pretty sure he works out because I saw muscles beneath his tailored suit the other day–"

"Of course you would notice that," Rose teased.

Mark made a sound of indignation. "Well, excuse me for admiring the wonderful masterpiece that is this man. If Astrid won't, then I certainly will."

I coughed, choking on my drink. Laughter broke out around me.

"I never said I wouldn't admire him," I shot back. "I'm just doing it from a safe distance."

He scoffed and patted me on the shoulder. "It's okay to take chances so they don't slip you by." He turned back to the table with a conspiratorial smile. "Besides, they *did* almost kiss in the vault."

"Which you still need to give us *all* the details about," Georgia declared, pointing at me and swaying slightly.

I chuckled. "I think you need to lay off the tea."

She waved at me. "Spill."

"As I said in my text, I tripped on a safety deposit box. He caught me. Next thing I knew, we were only inches apart with little space between us." I shrugged and tried to sound like it hadn't sent my heart racing, not just because of the fear of falling. "He may have glanced down at my lips…"

"Ooohh," the table echoed, and I blushed while swirling my drink.

"It was nothing."

"Bullshit! If he glanced at your lips, he definitely wanted to kiss you," Rose declared.

My blush deepened further. "I doubt that. We are coworkers. There are rules against that."

Mark scoffed. "Because that held you back with Asher."

"Asher was a mistake. One I don't intend to make again."

He raised his hands in surrender. "Fine. But when I'm right, you owe me a drink. Or two."

We all laughed.

I couldn't help but think, what if Mark *was* right? Ethan seemed like a decent enough guy, but I also didn't know much about him. Since that day in the vault, we had both seemed to be avoiding the other. Was it possible he had felt the same attraction and was keeping his distance for the same reason I was?

"Do you know why he moved here?" I suddenly blurted out.

Mark grinned triumphantly at me. "Thinking about him?" He waggled his brows.

I rolled my eyes. "Well, you did bring him up."

He laughed. "He moved here because he wanted to, I'm guessing. Some tellers have said he went through a bad divorce, and she left him and his daughter behind."

"Daughter?"

He nodded. "You didn't know?"

"No... I haven't talked to him since the vault incident."

"Probably because you both are avoiding each other. But I've seen the way he stares at you when you aren't looking. And you're just as bad."

"Yeah, okay. Now you're just blowing smoke up my ass."

He shrugged. "Have I ever lied to you?"

I stayed quiet. Because the answer was no. No, he never had. In fact, he'd always had an uncanny sense of things, ever since we were in high school. He had saved all of us from making big mistakes, but he also had tried to sway us from some, and we hadn't listened. Only to come back to him and tell him he was right. It was a joke between our group that he had more intuition than all of us girls combined.

"I didn't think so," he snarked.

Soon after, we took to the dance floor. Swaying my hips and feeling the bass thump in my chest, I closed my eyes and let the music sweep me away. My friends danced around me, and I felt like this was where I belonged: with my best friends by my side. I felt like I could take on the world so long as I had them. I was safe, loved, and accepted. There was nothing more that I could ask for.

We collapsed back at our table, our feet aching and our laughter bubbling as much as our drinks. I felt a comfortable buzz muddying my mind, and my cheeks hurt from smiling so much. I had needed this after the last couple of weeks. The girls and Mark always knew how to cheer me up.

"I'm going to head home," I yelled over the music.

"Aw, but the night's still young!" Rose yelled back.

"Yeah, but I have work in the morning."

She waved me off.

I hugged everyone, then stumbled to the doors. Maybe I had overdone it a little. I took a deep breath before opening the glass doors and stepping outside, the brisk night air slapping me across the face. It almost sobered me up. Almost.

Somehow, I made it home without a problem and got inside my apartment. My head was spinning now, and I unsteadily checked Lacey's food supply before making my way to the bedroom. I sent a text to the group, then collapsed into bed. I was ready to forget everything that had happened since Chloe had found me with Asher. Everything was a mess, and I was ready for a break.

Puppies & Exes

ETHAN

Since I wasn't home all the time to train Rosy, I told Sophia that we would take her to puppy training class while I was off for the weekend. Thankfully, there was a class this Sunday that we could take her to at the pet store. I told Sophia that she would be the main person training the pup, since it was hers, and she happily agreed. However, when we got there, she could barely hold onto the leash as Rosy wanted to dart after every other dog to see if they wanted to play.

"Rosy, heel," I commanded over and over again, tugging her to the training area.

"Rosy, sit," Sophia tried once we finally got her corralled into the blocked-off area.

The pup sat, but just barely. Her tail was wagging a mile a minute, and her whole body shook with excitement. I was just glad we had at least gotten her potty-trained and that she had used the bathroom before we came in. Otherwise, we would have a nasty mess on our hands. The other four pups in the group weren't much better off. They all looked anxious and ready to play.

"Welcome to Puppy School, everyone," a young lady announced as she came into the arena, smiling from ear to ear.

I groaned inwardly. I didn't have enough caffeine in my system for this.

"Today, we will teach you, the owner, how to train your puppies to sit, walk on a leash, roll over, and heel. I can see all of our furbabies are ready to play, but don't worry. We will direct their attention to our training, and they will do great!" She stepped over to a table laden with treats and gadgets. She held up a small plastic...thing. "This is a clicker." She pressed it together, and it clicked. "Your pups will soon recognize it as a signal for when they need to pay attention. Optionally, you can also snap your fingers, and it will do the same thing. Try snapping to get your pups' attention."

I looked down at Sophia, who shrugged.

"I don't know how to snap yet," she told me.

I chuckled. "That's alright."

I snapped my fingers, and Rosy perked her ears, her eyes going to me and her mouth snapping shut as she cocked her head. As soon as she figured I wasn't doing anything else, she looked away, panting and eager to play again. I glanced at Sophia, who shrugged.

"As you can see, puppies get curious when they hear a new sound. Everyone, grab a clicker and a handful of treats. But don't give them the treats just yet! We will use them throughout today, so tuck them away into a pocket or your hand."

Hours later, we had Rosy walking and listening to both

Sophia and me. She had learned quickly, which was no surprise given her breed. Sophia got a kick out of teaching her how to roll over and sit, per the instructor's guidelines. A few times, the poor pup had fallen over backwards trying to get to the treat instead of sitting, making Sophia burst out laughing.

When we got home, Sophia set to work continuing to train Rosy in the backyard. I chuckled watching her. Sometimes the puppy would listen, and other times she would run around, then come and crouch, wagging her tail and barking at Sophia.

"Now, listen here, Rosy!" Sophia commanded, a hand on her cocked hip. "You need to learn to be a good dog, and good dogs listen to their owners."

The pup yapped at her, her front paws on the ground.

"Rosy. Sit."

She laid down.

"No! I said *sit*, not *lay down*."

Rosy yipped at her and rolled over.

"Ugh! Rosy!"

The pup went running, Sophia chasing behind her.

"Rosy, heel!"

"Rosy, stop!"

Yapping followed by laughter filled the air, and I chuckled, shaking my head. I stepped outside to watch them. Sophia now had the rope toy, and they were playing tug-of-war.

"I think she just wants to play right now, Sophia," I told her.

She glanced over, tugging at the rope. Rosy pulled back, jerking her arm.

"But I need to train her," she complained.

"We all need breaks from time to time, sweetie. Just let her play, and you can work on training her some more later."

"Fine."

Next thing I knew, they were running around the yard

together, the rope hanging between them, while pure joy spilled from Sophia in the form of laughter and screaming. I watched them for a few minutes, glad that Sophia had a friend at home at the very least.

Her teachers had said she was settling in fine, but I worried about her as she had only mentioned making one friend so far. I had hoped she would have made at least one at school by now. Otherwise, she was doing well in school. She turned in her homework on time, put forth her best effort, and was helpful in class.

She *seemed* happy.

"Daddy!" Her calling out to me brought me from my thoughts. "Watch this!"

She was on her play set with Rosy behind her. As soon as I looked up, she slid down the slide, the pup going down right after her. She giggled and ran over to me.

"Did you see? Rosy went down with me!"

"I saw! What a silly pup," I said, smiling.

"What's for dinner? I'm hungry!"

"You are, are you?"

Sophia nodded. "Can we have sesame chicken?"

"Sure. I'll call it in."

"Hooray!"

Rosy yipped at the sound of her excitement, and they took off running again.

I was resting peacefully that evening when I heard barking. I groaned, rolling out of bed and stumbling down the hall towards Sophia's room when I heard a crash. Growling followed by more barks.

Now I was fully awake, and I grabbed for the bat that I had hanging on the wall from when I had been a slugger back in Logan. It was a heavy metal bat and could easily do some damage. Rosy stood in Sophia's doorway, hackles raised and focused on the main living area, growling, her little lips pulled back in a snarl. I peeked in. Sophia was still sound asleep.

"Good girl, Rosy," I whispered.

She stayed put as I walked past towards the living room, bat at the ready.

"Fuck," a whisper broke the silence before a muffled thud.

"Watch what you're doing, Fred," a harsh woman's whisper.

I peered around the corner to see two people: one clearly a woman and one that I assumed was Fred.

"You didn't say anything about this guy having so much stuff, Helena," he sniped back in a whisper.

I flicked on the light, and they both froze.

"Shit," Helena gasped, looking wide-eyed at me. "It-it's not what it looks like, Ethan."

"Really? Because it sure looks a lot like you and whoever the fuck this is just broke into my house," I snarled.

Rosy padded up to me, snarling quietly, and she barked once at them as though emphasizing my statement.

"Ethan, I just–"

"Save it. Get the fuck out of my house."

"Look, man, she just wants to–" the man started as he turned around.

I pointed my bat at him. "You have no room to talk. I don't know what she told you, but you are both here in the middle of the night after breaking in. I could easily get you both arrested for that alone. I will only say it once more: get. The fuck. Out."

The man raised his hands and began backing away toward the door. "You got it. I don't need no cops here. C'mon, Helena."

She looked between us, hesitating. "Ethan, I just need a little cash."

"What for? What have you done?"

Her eyes took on a scared look, and I knew. She had fallen far further than just needing alcohol. She was now dependent on it, if she hadn't even done something worse. I shook my head with disgust.

"Get out," I told her, pointing towards the door. "And if you *ever* cross my path again, you will be sorry."

Knowing she was defeated, she moved toward the door slowly. Once they were gone, I called the cops. I wouldn't have this happen again. I made it clear I didn't want to press charges, but I needed the police report for insurance records. They understood, but cautioned me and told me to up my security system.

I didn't rest easily that night. I slept on the couch, bat at my side, with Rosy on the ground next to me. She seemed on edge too, raising her head to look at the door for every little sound she heard, and making little huffs of warning. Tomorrow, I would be buying her the biggest bone I could find after work.

Tense Lunch Break

ETHAN

AFTER TALKING TO THE SCHOOL ABOUT THE BREAK-in last night and ensuring they would keep a close eye on Sophia, I finally made my way to work, calling the after-school care on the way. They assured me that they would keep her close by and make sure I was the only one allowed to pick her up. Anxiety flooded my system, but I did my best to tamp it down. It hadn't seemed like Helena was there to kidnap her, but I just couldn't take any chances. I didn't know how desperate she was. From the way she had been talking, it had sounded like she was just going to rob me, but this nagging sense told me that if I hadn't woken up, something else could have happened. Either Sophia would have woken up, or gone missing, or any number of things. The list was endless in my mind, and my priority was always to keep her safe.

I pulled into the parking lot and rested my head back on the headrest, letting my eyes close for a moment so I could compose myself. I couldn't let the thoughts run rampant in my head. Maybe I should call my therapist on my lunch break. Actually, even better, I would text him. I pulled out my phone but hesitated before sending the message. I knew what he would say. I just needed to hear it.

> **Ethan**
> I had a really rough weekend. The ex showed up and tried to get me to let her see Sophia. Then last night, she and some man she knew broke into my house. I don't know what her intentions were, but my mind is going wild.

I put my phone away, knowing I wouldn't get a response again for probably another hour, then entered the bank. The tellers were there already, setting up their stations, and I naturally looked for the petite blonde. It had become a ritual now. I spotted her, then quickly looked away before she noticed me.

Inwardly, I knew I was playing with fire. This internal attraction to her was dangerous, and it was making me borderline obsessive. It's not like I could do anything if she *weren't* here, and it wasn't any of my business either. Fuck, I was so screwed. I couldn't get her out of my mind, and the dreams I was having of her didn't help by any means. Maybe it was time to look for a different job... No. Definitely not. I rejected that thought immediately, knowing it would only make it worse. I was in too deep, but I didn't know what to do. I was trapped under her spell that she unknowingly put me in.

I glanced up again out of the corner of my eye while booting up my computer. She was holding her head. I frowned. Why was she holding her head? Was she crying? Internally, I panicked and wanted to see what was wrong. Externally, I fidgeted in my seat, knowing I shouldn't. I glanced over again. She was rubbing her temples. Okay, so not crying. Headache, more than likely. I breathed a sigh of relief, but then began wondering why she would have a headache.

Did she not sleep well? Or maybe she had been out too late last night? Had she been with someone?

Ugh.

This was hopeless.

I was hopeless.

I tapped my fingers on my desk. Fucking hell, this woman was in my head.

I glanced over again. She wasn't there. I turned completely, eyes roving the line for her. She wasn't anywhere to be seen. Then Mark looked over and caught my eye. A sly smile appeared across his lips, and he motioned towards the back. I guess someone had caught me after all... I tried to look confused, but he just rolled his eyes and shook his head.

Fuck.

Me.

I sighed and quickly turned my attention to my calendar. Well, he could know all he wanted. He could scheme all he wanted. He could—

"She's got a headache. Probably had a little too much last night," Mark whispered, and I nearly catapulted off my chair.

"W-What?" I asked, blinking as I tried to reign my heart back into my chest.

"Headache. Slight hangover?" Mark's eyebrow quirked. "You good?"

"Y-Yeah. Why are you telling me this?"

He scoffed. "Don't pretend with me. I've seen you staring. She's fine. We just helped her get over a rough week."

"By drinking?" It was my turn to scoff.

"No. By spending time with her besties. She honestly doesn't drink that much. Just enough to let loose. But I think she may have overdone it last night. She didn't have much to eat."

I blinked. Why was I entertaining this conversation? "Uh, okay. Well, it's none of my business, but I have some Tylenol she can have." I handed him the bottle, then pretended to be busy with my computer.

He took it with a chuckle, tipped the bottle to get a couple, and handed it back. "I'll let her know it's from you."

"No!" I said it a little too loudly, and a couple of heads turned towards us. I smiled, nodding at them, then repeated myself quietly. "No. Just..." I sighed. "Just give them to her so she can go about her day without being miserable."

He shrugged and sauntered towards the break room.

I groaned and put my head in my hands. It was bad enough having her in my mind nearly twenty-four-seven, but to have her best friend notice... Then a thought occurred to me. If Mark had noticed, then who's to say *she* hadn't noticed? Fuck, fuck, fuck.

No.

It was fine.

She couldn't have noticed. She was never looking when I found myself watching her with interest or accidentally glancing in her direction. In fact, she seemed completely uninterested in me. It was fine. Eventually, this weird fascination with her would pass, and I would move on.

Later that day, my stomach started grumbling, and I realized it was time for lunch. It had been a surprisingly busy Monday. For which I was grateful, because that meant I didn't have any downtime where Astrid would draw my attention. I slipped out of my desk and turned to Rosa, the other banker.

"I'm headed to lunch," I informed her.

She nodded. "See you in an hour."

I tapped her desk, then headed toward the break room. As soon as I opened the door, I stopped in my tracks. Astrid was there. And from the looks of it, she had just started her break as well. She sat on the couch with her legs pulled up, a plate of pizza on her lap, and a book in her hand.

I cleared my throat and went to the fridge to grab my left-over Chinese from the other night. Popping it in the microwave, I leaned against the counter and pulled out my phone to distract myself. I pretended not to notice how she looked up and shifted her position slightly—tried to ignore it.

"Uh, thank you for the Tylenol earlier," she said.

I glanced up. *Dammit, Mark.* "You're welcome."

She quirked her head, her eyes narrowing slightly. "How'd you know I had a headache?"

"I saw you holding your head and figured you had one."

"Oh. Well, thanks."

I nodded once. "Hangover?"

She grimaced. "Slight. More dehydration than anything. I don't like getting more than a slight buzz, but forgot to get a snack to balance it out."

So, she does drink. But doesn't seem to have a problem with it, unlike Helena. "Sorry to hear that. Hope you get to feeling better."

"Thanks."

The microwave beeped, signaling it was done, so I grabbed my food and made my way to the table, which was right next to where she was seated.

"How was your weekend?" she asked as she came to sit at the table.

I tried not to act surprised. *So much for ignoring each other.* "It was...stressful."

"Oh. What happened?" She put her book down, and I glanced at the cover. It looked like a fantasy novel involving dragons.

109

"Uh, my ex-wife somehow found out we had moved here, and wanted to meet with me. Turns out she was just needing money for..." I glanced up, then away, when her brown eyes threatened to draw me in. "Well, she needed money for her addictions. Last night, she broke into my house."

Astrid gasped. "Oh wow! That's daring!"

I nodded. "Our new puppy alerted me."

"Did you call the cops?"

"After she left." I sighed. "I didn't want to press charges. It's...complicated."

"That's understandable. She's the mother of your child. I'm sure you wouldn't want to explain to your kid that their mom is in jail..."

I looked up then, and her eyes met mine. They were soft, warm, inviting. A delicate brown that reflected on the slight smattering of freckles on her cheeks. A subtle pink began to form on them, and I realized I'd been staring for far longer than I should have. I quickly looked away.

"Yeah. Exactly." I cleared my throat. "Anyways. Other than maybe drinking a little too much, how was your weekend?"

"It was good. I got a cat."

"A cat?" I looked at her again and was captivated by the excitement in her eyes.

"Yeah! She's the cutest thing ever. Here, let me show you a picture." She pulled out her phone and then handed it over to me.

My hand brushed hers, and lightning bolts shivered down my arm and straight to my crotch. Dammit. I tried to focus on what was in front of me while thoughts flooded my mind. Her hand had been so soft... Cat. Calico. Orange and black. I wondered how her hand would feel around my... White chest. Yellow eyes.

"Yeah," I said, my voice choked. "Cute." I made sure our

VAULTED

hands didn't come into contact again as I handed her phone back. "What's her name?"

"Lacey."

"Fitting. The black looks like lace around the orange."

"That's what I thought, too!" She giggled, and the sound warmed me to my core. "I figured a cat was a good alternative."

"To what?" I quirked a brow at her.

I heard her take a sharp intake of breath. It was quiet. Subtle. I fought the slight smirk trying to come to the corner of my lips. Did my quirking a brow do that, or was she gasping about something else? Either way, I wanted to hear it again. For a much more...intimate reason.

My pants were getting tight. Good thing I was sitting at a table, and she couldn't see. That would be embarrassing.

"Uh, to...men," she said, tucking a strand of hair behind her ear and looking away.

I blinked a few times. "Men?" I chuckled. "What's wrong with men?"

"Well, I, uh... I haven't had very good... luck... dating."

Fuck she was adorable when she was flustered. I couldn't help the smirk that formed this time. When she glanced back my way, I noticed her glance down at my lips and the way she drew in her lower lip ever so slightly. Dammit. She was making this difficult.

Work.

Coworker.

I could do this.

"Well, I'm sorry to hear that," I whispered. "I'm sure there's someone out there for you."

She shrugged and whispered back, "Perhaps. I just haven't found him yet."

"Really? What are your requirements for Mr. Right that every man seems to fail at meeting?"

"Well. First of all, they should be single."

Check.

"Second, they should be attractive."

I caught her glance up into my eyes. *Check.*

"Third, they should be kind."

Check.

"And devoted."

Also check.

She shrugged. "As I said, I'm content just having my cat and me. It seems no man in Brantley can match that description. Or at least, not the ones that are attracted to me."

Okay, fuck this.

"You sure about that?" I asked, catching us both by surprise.

Her eyes widened, and her mouth made a delicate o-shape before she asked, "W-What do you mean?"

I took a deep breath. I was going to throw caution to the wind. I was tired of playing pretend and tired of holding myself back. It was clear that she was just as attracted to me as I was to her.

"Astrid," I started, keeping my voice low. I noticed her slight shiver. "I'm not going to lie to you. I see the way you are looking at me right now, and I know that whatever happened in the vault last week altered both our lives somehow. So, how about we go on a date and see where this goes?"

Should I Try?

ASTRID

To say I was surprised would be the least to describe what I was feeling. *Did he actually just ask me out on a date?* I blinked. I must be dreaming. That was it. I chuckled nervously.

"Excuse me, what?" I asked.

"Go on a date with me," he repeated.

Not a question. A statement. A challenge.

"Uh..." I started.

"Just say yes. We both want to, and you know it."

I blushed. He was a lot bolder than I gave him credit for.

And he was absolutely right.

I *did* want to date him and see where it went. I could see us going steady. Maybe even becoming more serious over time. I didn't mind that he already had a child, either. It actually made me even more attracted to him. I had always wanted kids one day. A little girl would be perfect. I could see us painting nails, doing our hair... A boy would be nice too, of course. I'd always heard they were sweet.

"Well?" he prodded, suddenly seeming anxious, and I realized I hadn't said anything for a few minutes.

"O-Okay."

His smile was breathtaking. I felt my breath hitch. I said yes... to a date... with Ethan. Holy shit.

"So, Friday after work?" he asked.

I nodded. "That works."

"Perfect."

Now I would have to work with him all week, and that little tidbit would be in the back of my mind. Lovely.

"Well, uh, enjoy the rest of your lunch," I said quickly and got up.

"You know, this doesn't have to be awkward," he whispered.

"What doesn't?"

"We are both adults. You don't have to run away."

I took a deep breath. "I'm not running away."

He cocked his eyebrow, and damn if it didn't have me wanting to grab him and kiss him. "Then what are you doing? Don't you still have fifteen minutes?"

"I, uh..." *Shit.*

"Sit down. We can count this as a first date, so that Friday isn't so tense."

I felt a blush rise up my neck and into my cheeks. "We're at work."

"And two coworkers can't talk and get to know one another?"

Well, he did have a point... I sat back down slowly. "Okay, fine. What do you want to know?"

"Well, what's your biggest goal in life?"

"I'm saving up to get an accounting degree, then I would like to become an accountant."

"Really? That's a good field to go into. Why accounting?"

"I like numbers and balance, which is what accounting is all about. Plus, I like working one-on-one with people. Some of my favorite customers are business owners."

"Would you want your own agency or would you apply for a job with one?"

"I think I would work with an agency for a bit to learn the ropes before venturing on my own."

"Smart move."

"What about you?"

He shrugged. "I'm happy being a banker. I would eventually like to move into management, but it's not a necessity."

I cocked my head. "Have you always wanted to be a banker?"

He laughed. "No. I wanted to be a doctor when I was younger, but when I got married and had Sophia, my plans kind of changed."

"That makes sense. Kids are a big life decision."

"They are. Do you want kids?"

I nodded. "One or two. Not too many. How old is your daughter?"

"Six and she's got a mind of her own, but a huge heart."

I smiled. "She sounds lovely."

"She's my whole world."

I could see the adoration in his eyes, and it made me swoon. I loved how much he clearly cared for his daughter. It told me that he also had a big heart, one capable of love and understanding. One of dedication and truth. Or at least, I hoped so.

"Well, my fifteen minutes are up," I said as a timer went off on my phone. "Enjoy the rest of your lunch."

"Chat with you soon?" he asked.

"On the line?"

He nodded.

"I-I guess."

He gave me a lopsided grin. "I'll see you shortly then."

I blushed before walking away. If he used all the time at work to get to know me, what on earth were we going to talk about on Friday? Typically, dates were how you got to know one another. Not work. I felt off-kilter with this. He was so eager and...attentive. I found it both attractive and disarming.

"You look befuddled. Everything okay?" Mark asked as I stepped back into my window.

I leaned over to whisper, "Ethan just asked me on a date."

"Well, it's about damn time."

"Shh, keep your voice down."

He chuckled. "I was about to lock you two into a room if he didn't ask you sooner than later."

"Mark!"

"I'm serious! All the secret staring, goo-goo eyes, and casual glances. It was getting ridiculous."

I groaned.

"Soooo. Did you say yes?"

I nodded.

"Yes! Atta girl!"

"Shh!"

"Sorry. I'm just so excited. You guys are perfect for each other."

"For once, I hope your intuition is spot on and not just coincidental."

"Oh, honey. I'm *always* right.'

"Not always. There was that time when John–"

"We don't need to talk about him."

I snickered.

"So when's the date?"

"Well..."

"Ash. Don't leave me hanging."

"Technically, we just had our first one, according to him?"

"Astrid Hart! Explain!"

"Well, he asked me, and I was going to escape, because I felt really awkward, but he told me to sit. Then we started talking..."

He leaned on the counter between us. "About what?"

"Well, he asked what my biggest goal was, and I asked about his daughter."

He grinned. "So nothing surface level. That's great!"

"And he said that we could keep talking while here at work." I blushed.

Mark chuckled. "He's so desperate. It's adorable."

"Desperate?"

"Oh, honey. You have *no* idea the looks he has been giving you. I dare say that boy has been dreaming of you since the vault incident."

I scoffed. "I doubt that."

I had to look away from him as my thoughts began to run wild. What exactly kind of looks *had* he been giving me that would make Mark claim such a thing? I guess, one day, if and when we got to know each other better, I could ask. Until then, I could only wonder.

"You'll see. I know I'm right," Mark commented.

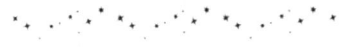

Half an hour later, Ethan came off his lunch break. He gave me a smile before retreating to his desk. I felt a little disappointed but, at the same time, relieved. He had a job to do, after all. We both did. We couldn't just spend our whole shift talking to each other.

Later on, though, he did come to stand behind me on the teller line. His presence was felt more than seen. My whole being was attuned to it as I helped a customer. I could feel his stare behind me, even though I was certain he was probably not even staring directly at me the entire time. I wasn't conceited like that. Once the customer left, he stepped closer.

"Where do you want to go on Friday?" he asked in a hushed tone.

I glanced at Mark, who was paying attention but not making it obvious.

"Isn't the guy supposed to pick the place?" I returned in a tone matching his.

"Touché." He grinned, making my heart skip a beat. "I'm still new to town, so I'd like to know what you would suggest."

"Well, I like Midnight Society, but–"

A strange look crossed his features.

"What?"

"I'd prefer not to go to a bar."

"Oh. Okay. That's fine. How about Italian then?"

"Italian is good."

I nodded. "Okay. There's a place called Gusto Italiano, and they are pretty good. Or there is a small Italian cafe called Nonna's. It's not as popular, but the food is amazing."

"Nonna's sounds good."

I bit my lip and nodded again. "Okay."

I didn't miss his glance down at my lip, and I released it. The heat in his gaze became too much, so I turned away. Maybe Mark had been right. There was just way too much in that one look that had me thinking of all the dirty things we could do... But I didn't want to go there. Not yet. I wanted to take this slow.

I heard him take in a deep breath behind me.

It was going to be a long, tantalizing week.

Mark
Guess who has a date on Friday!

Rose
You? With what's his name? Gareth?

Mark
Nope! Astrid!

Georgia
I thought she was wanting to be single for awhile?

Astrid
Guys... I'm in the chat, too, ya know...

Daisy
Oh, leave the poor girl be! (But who's it with?)

Mark
Ethan! The new banker I've been telling you all about.

Astrid
STILL HERE!

Georgia
WHAT?! I need the tea!

Mark
They're going to Nonna's on Friday

Astrid
OMG... You couldn't wait, could you?

Mark
No. I need everyone to know when I'm right. Which I usually am

Astrid
Ugh... You're insufferable

Mark
But that's why you all love me XOXO

Rose
Lol

Daisy
I mean, he isn't ALWAYS right. There was that time with John

Mark
WE DON'T TALK ABOUT JOHN

Georgia
🎵We don't talk about Bruno, no, no, no 🎵

Rose
🎵We don't talk about Bruno🎵

Mark
UGH

Astrid
Lol. We DO love you, Mark

Mark
I know 💋

The next day, I couldn't decide what to wear to work. I fought between trying to appease Ethan's tastes, whatever they were, and wearing what *I* wanted to wear. For so long, I had worn what I thought would be attractive to the opposite sex, namely Asher, when it came to work, that it was now an internal battle. I reminded myself that I wouldn't be that girl anymore and reached for a maxi skirt and matching top.

I didn't need to impress anyone. If Ethan didn't like me for who I was, it was better to know now than after I had fallen for him. It would hurt much less.

My usual morning routine before work had altered somewhat since getting Lacey. Now, instead of showering, getting dressed, then getting a coffee, I checked her litter box and gave her some food before making my coffee. Then, while it was brewing, I would snuggle with her for a bit on the couch. I went through this new ritual and sat with a purring Lacey on my lap.

"I'm really anxious about work today," I confessed to her as she purred on my lap. "This guy, Ethan, wants to go on a date on Friday, but he wants to get to know me during work, too. It's a little nerve-racking."

She looked up at me and grunted.

"What? It is."

She meowed and turned away.

"I know. I know. I should care less and be myself, but I just... I want someone to love me for me."

She purred loudly and brushed her head against my hand. And I realized I was talking to a cat as if she could understand me. I chuckled, shook my head, and got up to get my coffee.

"Alright, Lacey. Be good while I'm gone," I told her before heading to the bank.

Ethan's truck was already there. My heart began to race with anticipation, and nervous energy washed over me. I couldn't believe I was actually going on a date with a coworker. An *actual* date. Not a booty call. I took a deep breath before getting out of my car and heading inside. I could do this. I could be brave.

I grabbed my box from the vault and began setting up my window. Just like every other day. The only difference? I was now keenly aware of the banker across the lobby. Every move he made had me glancing over from the corner of my eye, unsure of when he would be coming to stand along the teller line.

It wasn't until the day was well underway that he came over, standing behind Mark and me like it was the most normal place to be. He waited until the customer at my window had left before leaning against the counter separating Mark and me, maintaining a respectful, appropriate distance.

"I've done some thinking," he stated.

Uh-oh, here it comes. I turned to face him after giving Mark a 'here we go' look. My stomach sank as I anticipated his canceling Friday's plans.

"About?" I asked.

He gave me his lopsided grin. "Can I get your number?"

I blinked in surprise. "Oh."

"Oh?" He quirked a brow.

"I mean, yes. Yeah. Of course."

"What did you think I was going to say?"

I blushed and turned away to grab my sticky note pad and a pen. Jotting down my number, I tore off the note and handed it to him.

"I'm not sure," I replied. "I guess I expected you to cancel Friday."

He chuckled as he tucked the number into his pocket. "No. I very much plan on still taking you out."

"Good grief. You guys are ridiculous," Mark mumbled.

"How are things with your daughter?" I asked Ethan, ignoring Mark's comment.

"Good. I got a new security system installed yesterday, so I can sleep a little better now," Ethan replied. "And the school and after-school care know only to allow me or my friend James and his wife Leora to pick her up."

"That's good to hear."

"What is your favorite flower?"

I had to think about that. Although Daisy owned a flower shop, I hadn't really given much thought to flora, nor which one would be my favorite. However, I did remember one that was particularly beautiful.

"I would have to say the orchid," I answered finally.

He nodded to himself. "Good to know. And your favorite holiday?"

"Easy, New Year's."

He quirked a brow. "New Year's?"

I nodded. "You get to start fresh and reevaluate your life so you can learn from the mistakes of years past while making resolutions for the future. It's an opportunity to make the year better than before. Start fresh with a clean slate, so to speak."

"That's...a very smart way of thinking about it. Most people say Christmas, or Thanksgiving."

"And what is your favorite?"

"Valentine's Day."

I blinked in surprise, not having expected that. "Why?"

"It's romantic." He grinned. "I have a romantic soul, believe it or not."

"Do you now?"

He nodded.

"And what is romance to you?"

"Candlelit dinners. Picnics. Walks in the moonlight." He lowered his voice. "Time spent with someone you appreciate."

I realized I'd been holding my breath and had been staring. I quickly looked away, breaking whatever spell I had been under.

"Well, that sounds lovely," I commented.

"It was supposed to sound appealing." He chuckled.

"Well, we will see."

"You sound like you doubt it."

"In my experience, people can say whatever they like. It is whether they follow through or not that truly matters."

"Ouch." He put a hand to his chest. "I understand what you mean, but I can't say I've ever been on the receiving end of skepticism."

I gave him an apologetic smile before quietly saying, "I've been burned too many times to count."

I felt bad, but at the same time thought it was something he should know. After all, he would know all my faults soon enough if things went well. Figured it best to get the biggest out of the way to see if he would run for the hills or take the challenge.

"Well, sounds like I will have to prove to you that I am different from the rest, then," he replied.

"Good luck with that," Mark commented.

Ethan glanced at him, then back at me, and quirked a brow. "I may need some context."

I shook my head. "I prefer to leave the past where it belongs: in the past. That doesn't mean I don't learn from it, though."

"Fair enough. It's good to learn from our mistakes."

I scoffed. "I never said they were *my* mistakes."

"Some of them were," Mark butted in.

I glared at him. "Yes. *Some* were."

Ethan looked between us. "Well... It's good to forgive and move forward, even if it's ourselves that we are forgiving."

I smiled at him gratefully.

"What hobbies do you have?"

"Well, I like to read—a lot. So I like to visit the bookstore quite often. Or the library." I thought a bit more. "Uh, I also like to go on hikes in the mountains from time to time. Nature relaxes me."

He nodded. "Nature is a good cure-all for when you're stressed or just needing some peace."

"Exactly." I smiled broadly while Mark scoffed.

"If you like going on hikes, why'd you get a cat and not a dog?"

"I would feel bad making it wait to use the bathroom or for leaving it alone all day. Dogs are such needy, lovable creatures. I knew a cat would still love me even if I left it alone all day."

Ethan laughed. "My daughter's pup apparently never got that memo."

I blushed in embarrassment.

He noticed, his eyes going wide as he raised his hands. "Not saying that you don't have a point. Dogs are much more attached to their owners than cats are."

"*Most* cats are that way. My tomcat is very clingy and needy," Lola, the branch manager, commented as she walked by. "Y'all are some chatty Cathy's today. Good to see you all getting along and bonding. I hope to see some teamwork out of it!"

I grinned while I felt butterflies start fluttering in my stomach. We were being too noticeable. If work caught on that Ethan and I were seeing each other... That was preposterous. We weren't going steady. Just getting to know one another. Just like any coworkers who were new to working together would. Nothing wrong with that. Right?

Date Night

ASTRID

FRIDAY HAD ARRIVED.

And I was an anxious mess.

Okay. That was an understatement.

I was nervous, excited, and my stomach felt like I was on the verge of throwing up.

Lacey paced around my ankles, rubbing against me and purring as loud as she could, almost like she could sense how I was feeling and was trying to gain my attention so she could comfort me. I reached down to pet her, and her head bumping against my hand was borderline aggressive. I chuckled.

"I'm alright, Lace. Just a little nervous about my date, but I'm sure it'll be just fine," I told her.

All week, Ethan and I had been getting to know one another whenever we had the chance. Our questions ranged from our favorite things to what annoyed us the most to what we thought the meaning of life was. Okay, kidding on the last one, but sometimes they would get a little philosophical and deep. Much deeper than any other conversation I'd had with another man. He was easy to talk to, understanding, and truly listened. It really baffled me that his ex-wife had left him. He couldn't be perfect. Something had to be wrong with him.

He did have a daughter.

If things got serious between us, was I ready to be a mother right off the bat? What if she didn't like me? What if I couldn't fulfill the role that Ethan would need me to fill? Did he want me to fill it? My head started to hurt, and I groaned, leaning my head back and closing my eyes.

What was I getting myself into? Just because I felt an innate attraction to him that left me absolutely breathless did not mean I could become a decent mother to his child overnight. Let alone one she would like. I knew next to nothing about being a mother. My own had been hot and cold, distant then so overbearing that I thought I would suffocate. She went from hardly a slap on the wrist to throwing away prized possessions or calling me a bitch because 'I was crying too loud and would wake my sister.'

Memories of my childhood flooded my mind, and I had to work on steadying my breathing. *In. Out. In. Hold. Out.* I felt my body starting to relax once again.

It wasn't that I had a *bad* childhood, necessarily. Just one that wasn't consistent.

I refused to be like that towards a child, my own or anyone else's. Children ought to be protected and shown their value. I just didn't know how to do that. I was sure I could learn. I *would* learn. It would become necessary if Ethan and I got more serious. I would even take classes on how to be a mother if I had to. Or read books. That seemed more like my learning venue, anyway. I would give it a month, maybe two. Or perhaps I could start learning now.

I shrugged. For now, I needed to focus on getting ready for work. I was already overthinking this more than necessary. It would work out, or it wouldn't. Either way, it was better to love than to never love at all. Or in this case, never try.

As I searched my closet for something I could wear not only to work, but to Nonna's for our date, my mind began to whirl again. Was I ready to try dating again? It felt like just yesterday I had sworn off men and gotten Lacey instead. Yet, that was almost a week ago now. I shook my head. Ethan was my last-ditch effort. If he turned out to be a dud like the rest, I would officially take a break.

I pulled out a pair of high-waisted black slacks, a plain white tee, and a shiny, thin black belt. Tucking in the shirt, I pulled out the edges just slightly, then slipped the belt through the loops on the slacks and fastened it. It was casual, but chic. A perfect outfit for work, then going to the quaint Italian restaurant after. I tugged on my black pea coat before grabbing my purse and keys.

"I'll be home later, Lacey," I told her as she crouched by her food to nibble.

I gave her a quick pet then left, making sure to lock the door behind me. On my drive to work, I pumped myself up. Everything would work out, one way or another. With or without Ethan, I would be fine. I could handle life on my own. I had for the last decade, and I certainly could for another. It wasn't like I *needed* a man. They were nice, but I had my friends to lean on when I needed someone. My phone dinged, and I smiled, already knowing it would be one of the gals or Mark. I pulled it out at a stoplight.

> **Rose**
> Are you ready for your date with the hot banker?? 😉

I rolled my eyes before typing a response.

> **Astrid**
> Yes, but nervous.

Daisy
It'll be alright! You got this! Just be yourself

Astrid
Always

Georgia
Good luck!

Mark
And we want to know EVERYTHING once you get home. And I do mean everything!

I laughed aloud.

Astrid
Of course

The workday droned on for what seemed like forever. Or maybe it was just because I was ready for it to be over. Ethan seemed a little more distant than usual, and it made me even more anxious. Or maybe I was just reading into it. He was still his usual, friendly self whenever he came around. So surely it was just me.

It had to be.

I was being extra sensitive because of my nerves and was anticipating the other shoe to drop. However, I knew the facts: he was divorced, so I couldn't be the other woman. He had confirmed our date last night, so I knew he wasn't going to bail at the last minute. I just needed to chill, plain and simple.

Finally, the end of the day came. We had agreed to take separate vehicles to Nonna's so that people wouldn't talk at work. It was best if we lay low. Not that we were keeping secrets, but we knew it was better to be discreet.

As I pulled into the parking lot of Nonna's, I gave myself a pep talk. Ethan and I had already done much of the small talk at work. Yes, we would be alone for the first time since the vault, but that was okay. We were only trying it out. It didn't mean anything serious. I nodded to myself, then headed inside.

Ethan was already waiting, and he smiled as I walked up. "There you are. I was afraid you got lost."

I chuckled. "Lost? I'm the one who told you how to get here, remember?"

"Oh, I remember. But I thought that was a nicer way of questioning why you took longer to come inside." He winked as I felt a blush creep up my cheeks. "It's okay. I'm nervous, too."

I opened my mouth to ask why, but was cut off as the hostess took us to our seats. I settled in, glazing over the menu. I already knew what I wanted, having looked over, debated, and reasoned with myself about each dish during my lunch break. Still, I didn't want to seem too decisive or prepared, so I glanced over it for a time before setting it down.

Ethan ordered us a bottle of wine to share with our meals, then turned to me, "Do you want an appetizer?"

"No, I'm alright, thank you," I replied.

I doubted I could even stomach the main dish at this

point, let alone an appetizer. We sat for a while, silent and uncomfortable. I shifted in my seat.

"Do—" I began just as he said, "Are—"

We laughed.

"Go ahead," he offered, motioning towards me.

"Do you believe in fate?"

He blinked, then smirked at me. "Well, that's an interesting question to lead with."

I took a sip of my wine to hide the blush forming on my cheeks. Perhaps it had been a little too forward a question, but he had mentioned being a romantic, so I was curious.

"Yes, I believe in fate, to a degree. I think we all have choices, but I do think that there are times when our fate is sealed, no matter what."

"For example?"

He paused to think a moment. "Well, I think that my meeting Sophia's mom wasn't an accident. I believe that was fate; otherwise, Sophia wouldn't be here. And I believe that eventually I will meet someone destined to be her true mother, if I haven't already."

I shrugged. "Or perhaps that was just a chance."

He smiled. "Perhaps. But I'd like to think that Sophia would have happened, regardless."

"You love her a lot."

"She *is* my daughter; I should hope I love her."

I chuckled. "What I mean is that some parents would... hold it against their children that the marriage didn't work out, even if not intentionally. Or they may resent them because they remind them of the other parent. It's nice to see that you have a healthy, loving relationship, at least from what I can tell from how you talk about her."

He nodded. "I know what you mean. I spent a year in therapy to help me heal, but I never wanted her to feel that she wasn't loved or unworthy of love. She's only a child. It's not her fault that her mother chose the bottle over her family."

I winced. *So that's why he said no to Midnight Society.* It made sense now. He must have a bad taste in his mouth for bars and clubs. Though I was glad to see he was okay with socially drinking. Or was he possibly testing me? Seeing if I would get drunk? I couldn't blame him, but I would like to think he would discuss it first.

"Sorry if that sounded harsh," he commented quietly.

I shook my head quickly. "No need. I understand. I'm guessing that's why you wanted something more...formal."

He sighed. "I don't have a problem with drinking, so long as it is done responsibly and within limitations, if that makes sense."

"Perfectly." I paused, thinking over my following words carefully before deciding to go for it. "I hope I didn't put you on edge by suggesting Midnight Society at first."

"No. I know it's popular around here. I just..."

I held up my hand. "You don't have to explain. I understand."

He gave a small smile.

The waitress came back and took our orders. I was glad for the slight break in our heavy conversation. I was trying to think of a way to lighten it when I remembered he had also tried asking a question when I had.

"What was it you were going to ask?" I asked, then took a sip of wine.

"Oh, I was going to ask if you are more like your mother or your father," he replied.

I chuckled. "I don't know about my father, but I have similarities to my mother. However, I have taken some of her behaviors and improved them, and there are some that I definitely will change in my own life."

"What do you mean?"

"Well, she wasn't the best mother." I grimaced. "Without trauma dumping, I would like to be more present and more consistent with my children. Make sure they know they are loved no matter what, you know?"

He grinned. "Completely."

The waitress brought our food out, refilled our water, and then left.

"Wow, these look amazing," Ethan commented.

"Wait till you try it," I replied with a small laugh.

He took a bite of his Alfredo and closed his eyes. "Oh, wow. I'm so glad you suggested this place."

I chuckled as I took a bite of my chicken saltimboca. "It's definitely one of the better restaurants in Brantley." I swallowed. "So, what about you?"

"Hm?"

"Are you more like your mother or father?"

"I would say I'm a healthy mix of both. My mother was very loving and nurturing. My father is firm, but also loving. He also has a wicked sense of humor and is a romantic as well. I have very fond memories of them dancing in the kitchen or him bringing home flowers, especially if he happened to get into an argument with my mom." He chuckled. "She was quite stubborn."

"Was?"

"She passed away a couple of years ago."

"Oh, I'm sorry. I shouldn't have asked."

"That's alright." He smiled. "I like that I'm able to remember her." His phone rang, and he quickly set down his fork to retrieve it. He smiled apologetically. "I'm sorry. I have to get this."

My heart sank slightly. Was this where things came crashing down? Who was calling him? I nodded as he stood and rushed to the entrance to answer his phone. He talked animatedly to whoever was on the other line, and I saw his shoulders droop as his brow furrowed. Was that worry or frustration? Guilt? My mind began to go a mile a minute. Did he already have a girlfriend, and was that who was calling him? Asking him where he was? He made his way back and flagged down our waitress.

"Astrid, I'm so sorry, but I have to cut our date short. Sophia caught the flu," he said, his face genuinely apologetic.

Was that some excuse? I couldn't fight the plaguing thoughts while also feeling guilty for second-guessing him. I nodded.

"I understand," I told him.

He paid the bill, boxed up his food, and was gone within minutes, leaving me behind wondering if it was just some elaborate excuse. I felt bad for feeling this way, but I couldn't help but feel he was just like the rest of the men in Brantley.

What Now?

ETHAN

AFTER REGRETFULLY LEAVING ASTRID AT NONNA'S, I rushed home. Leora had called me, saying Sophia had started throwing up and was running a fever. She assured me she could stay until I finished our date, but I knew that Sophia would feel much better if I were home with her. The last thing I wanted her to feel was that going on a date was more important than her. I would have to make it up to Astrid some other time.

I could tell she had been disappointed. Her eyes had dimmed, their excited light going dark. I truly hoped she would forgive me and let me have another chance. For some reason I couldn't explain, I just knew she was the one I had been looking for. Her comments about wanting to be a better mother showed how much she cared and that she was willing to learn how to be a good mom. Her understanding of my issues with going to a bar showed that she was level-headed and reasonable. I had misjudged her when I had first seen her on that dating app, and now I regretted not giving her the chance early on.

Shame on me for judging a book by its cover. I should've known better.

I pulled into the garage and hurried to Sophia's room. She was asleep, but a bowl sat on her nightstand, along with a bottle of ginger beer and a stack of saltines.

"She just fell back asleep," Leora whispered as she pulled on her jacket and purse.

"I am so sorry. I hope you don't get sick," I whispered back.

She smiled. "Don't worry about me. I'll take an immunity shot when I get home. It's that time of year!"

I nodded. "Yeah. I just hate when she catches it."

Leora patted me on the shoulder. "She will be alright. She's a tough one. How did your date go?"

"Well, we had just started eating when you called."

She shook her head. "I told you that you could have finished your date, Ethan. You don't get to get out much."

"No, no. I need to be here for her."

Leora sighed. "Ethan. I know you want to be a good dad, but don't forget that you have needs, too. I hope that girl understands."

"I think she will."

Her eyes volleyed between my own as a sly smile crept across her face. "You like her."

I looked away. "It's too early to tell."

She bumped my shoulder. "Text her at least. Make sure she doesn't think you bailed for no reason."

I nodded, but as soon as she left, Sophia was throwing up again, and I completely forgot to text Astrid.

It took almost half a week for Sophia to start feeling better. In the meantime, I had texted Astrid, only to be met with silence. Worry and dread had plagued me for the first couple of days. Had I been right about her? Was she not as understanding as she had let on? Once the anxiety had passed, the frustration came. She was just like the lot of them. All women here and in Logan seemed to be cut of the same cloth – only interested in a man to have a good time with and not one to settle down with. Well, she could find that elsewhere. I didn't have time or energy to waste on someone who wasn't ready.

It was the following Wednesday when I finally returned to work. I wasn't sure what to say to her or what to do when I ran into her. A different kind of anxiety filled me. Uncertainty and frustration a toxic combination pulsing through my mind and system. I had to face her, one way or another.

I took a deep breath before entering the bank building. Then I walked past the teller line and straight towards my desk without another look. If she wanted to ignore me, fine. I would give her her space, and we could move on as if nothing had happened.

My heart pained in my chest in disagreement.

I tried to ignore it. There was no reason for it to be doing that. It's not like I was *in love* with her. Not already. There was no way I could be.

I glanced over, and the way my heart skipped a beat when I spied her told me otherwise.

I quickly looked away before anyone could see me looking over.

I had never felt this way toward anyone, not even Sophia's mother. It couldn't be infatuation. I was altogether familiar with that, having had many crushes in my school years to now. No, this was deeper. More innate. More consuming.

It didn't matter.

She made it very clear that she wasn't interested, and I would have to deal with that.

Somehow, I would have to work my way through the devastation that was quickly eating away at me as I realized I had fallen in love with her before I had even noticed it happening, let alone reel in the feelings before they had taken over. Somehow, I would have to do that and still maintain our business relationship while not falling deeper in love with someone I couldn't have. Somehow, I would have to move on from this.

Maybe it was time to make an appointment with my therapist...

Later that day, I sat in my truck with my phone on speaker. My therapist, Hank, was on the other line as he listened to me explain all things Astrid to him.

"Wow, man. Sounds like you really have it in for this girl," he commented.

I groaned and rested my head back against the headrest. "Yeah, I do. And that's the problem. She ghosted me. And we work together. I don't know what to do now."

He was silent for a time. "Well, you need to show that you respect her decision as hard as that is. I know you really want to find a mom for Sophia and a partner for life, but it might be time to focus on just you and your daughter while you adjust to living in a new city."

"So you're saying I'm rushing things again?"

"I didn't. You did."

I smiled, knowing exactly what he was doing. "So that's a yes."

"It's okay to take on one thing at a time, that is all I'm saying. If you concluded that you are rushing, then your subconscious may be trying to communicate that to you."

"I think my subconscious is still in love with a girl I can't have, and it decided to fall for her before I even knew what was going on."

"Maybe. You know yourself better than I do, so you know what to do. You need to stop fighting yourself on it."

I sighed, knowing he was right. Yes, I had instantly fallen for Astrid without knowing it, but I had also rushed into it as well. I could have saved the getting-to-know-each-other for later, after we officially went on a date. I could have called her in the evenings after Sophia had fallen asleep. Instead, I had mixed work with pleasure, making it awkward for both of us, more than likely.

I needed to respect that she was either not interested or wanted space. Either way, she clearly had no intention of talking to me, so I needed to give her that. You couldn't force something on someone if they didn't want it.

"It's also possible that this girl may not be ready to settle down," Hank interrupted my thought process. "She may be close in age, but she doesn't have any kids of her own, right?"

"Right."

"And no serious relationships, that you know of?"

"No."

"So it's possible that she isn't ready. She may come back around later, after she has her fun being a single lady and all the freedom that entails. Time will tell."

"Yeah. You're right."

"I know I am. Now, how are you going to manage all of this?"

"Shove it down and call it a day?"

He was silent for a moment, and when I didn't say anything, he sighed, "You know what I'll say to that."

I chuckled. "Work myself to death."

"Ethan..."

"I'm joking." I paused. "I'll manage my emotions by focusing on work, keeping myself healthy, and giving her the space she is asking for. I'll keep myself in check and maintain a business-level relationship, if we ever are around each other."

"Good plan. Let me know if you need another meeting to talk through anything."

"You got it. Thanks, Hank."

"Anytime."

We hung up, and I went back to work, feeling lighter and more determined.

Even if Astrid was like the other girls, I knew I would be okay. I still had Sophia. I still had my job. And I could manage to work near Astrid every day. After all, our relationship hadn't been serious by any means. It was nice getting to know her, but now it's time to treat her like any other coworker.

I slipped behind the teller line and made my way past her station towards the center. As I did, I caught a whiff of her vanilla and cardamom scent, instantly sending my stomach into somersaults and getting rock hard. I discreetly adjusted myself behind an empty station, acting like I was looking at the slips to make sure they were in stock, or something. It was going to be a while before her scent didn't affect me anymore. Until then, it was going to be hard to work around her.

I skimmed over the line, trying to appear as casual as possible, and caught her gaze. For a moment, our eyes met and held. My heart galloped in my chest, and I noticed a blush creep along her cheeks before she looked away. There had been something in her eyes. Surprise? Regret? Something, but I couldn't tell what from this distance.

Her friend Mark spotted me and shrugged. Apparently, even our matchmaker didn't know the cause of her silence. Or so it would seem. Maybe I could pick his brain later when

Astrid took her break. If he would even tell me anything, though, it would be a miracle as he was her best friend, and I knew better than to ask him to spill her secrets. I also wouldn't ask him to.

An hour later, she left for her break, and I casually made my way over to Mark. I knew he knew I was there, so I waited for him to start any conversation he wanted to have.

He turned around after a customer left and started with, "So, what *actually* happened?"

I raised a brow in confusion. "What?"

"She said you left her mid-date. Instead of assuming, I'm asking for your side of the tale."

"My daughter got the flu. I had to go home to take care of her."

"No other woman, and not a fake excuse?"

"Of course not. I don't believe in leading people along or lying. Honesty is the best policy out there, and I abide by it."

He nodded once. "I thought so, but I had to confirm. She is really struggling with it right now."

"What do you mean?"

He looked around to make sure no one would eavesdrop before he lowered his voice, "She's had pretty bad luck with guys the last few months. The first guy she dated for quite some time kept promising to break up with his girlfriend, but never did. Then the two guys after that were either married or engaged. So she has some trust issues when it comes to guys, and when you had to bail, which I'm not saying you didn't have a reasonable reason as to why, she started to question everything."

"She didn't even give me the opportunity to prove her wrong."

"No, she didn't. Which I've been badgering her about, believe me."

I could see the sincerity in his eyes and found myself

believing him. Even if he wasn't my friend, I knew he had her best interests in mind.

"So what do you recommend then?" I asked.

He shrugged. "Give her some time. She's battling with her mind right now."

I nodded. "Thanks, man."

Patience would be my game. I just hoped my dreams wouldn't plague my mind again.

Locked In

ASTRID

I NEEDED MONEY IN MY TILL.

The only problem was that the other banker and my manager were on lunch, leaving only Ethan available to help me get cash. I would be pushing my luck if I didn't swap out the larger bills for smaller ones now. So with a sigh, I closed my window to balance my till and get everything ready so that the vault exchange would be as quick as possible.

"Hey, Ethan," I called over once I was ready.

He looked up almost immediately and sauntered over. Each step closer sent my heart racing, and butterflies took flight in my stomach once he was at my station.

"Yes?" his deep voice seemed to caress me.

"I, uh," I stalled, breathless, and cleared my throat to continue. "I need to make an exchange for smaller bills from the vault."

"Alright, let's take a look."

He stepped into my window as I moved aside, his body brushing slightly against mine in the tight area. I felt my core clench. I couldn't stop how my body reacted to him, even if my mind was racing with thoughts of how he wasn't the right one for me. Mark and I had argued over it this morning. He insisted I had everything wrong and that I give the guy a chance. Maybe I should. But then again, how did I know if he was telling the truth?

After our date, Ethan had texted me a few times, asking if he could make it up to me. But my mind was still confused and muddled with thoughts of the other duds I had dated, so I couldn't think clearly about it. All I could see were their lies. It wasn't fair to him, I knew that, but it also didn't feel right for me to go forward while I doubted him. Mark insisted I just needed to move on, let all that go, and give Ethan at least a chance to talk to me about it. It wasn't until my lunch that I decided that I could do that.

I followed Ethan to the vault after locking everything up. Anxiety coursed through my veins. What if he tried to talk about it now? Would he be willing to wait until after work? Would he even bother talking to me after I had ghosted him for almost a week? Personally, I wouldn't. I would write the person off and move on.

As we stepped into the vault, it began to feel like the walls were closing in on me as my anxiety blossomed into a monster I could no longer hide. Breathing became difficult, and my vision became crowded with black. I tried to focus on my breathing as Ethan turned around. His brows knit in confusion, then widened with panic when he realized what was happening.

"Hey, hey," he soothed. "What's wrong? Breathe, Astrid. In. Then out."

As I followed his instructions, I heard a metallic clang behind me.

"Shit." He was looking past me.

I turned to see that the vault door had somehow closed behind us.

We were locked in.

My calm breathing began to increase again.

"Hey, no, it's okay," he said, grabbing my shoulders and turning me around.

The lights dimmed.

The power was out. We were locked in the vault. And we were running on backup power.

Ohfuckohfuckohfuck.

"Breathe, Astrid." Ethan was in front of me again, his face right in front of mine as he rested his forehead against mine. "In. Hold. Out."

I followed his breathing and felt myself begin to level out. He was so close to me. So close he could kiss me if he wanted to. Then he backed away, and I was shocked by the bereft feeling that consumed me.

"Well, this is quite the turn of events," he commented.

I looked around us in the dim lighting before whispering, "I'll say."

There was a moment of tense silence.

"Astrid, I-" he started and paused as I turned to face him.

"What?" I asked.

He was only a foot away from me. Close enough that I could feel his body heat, but far enough that it was clear he was either distancing himself or trying to give me space.

"I'm sorry I had to leave our date early. Sophia was really sick, and I didn't want her to feel like she was less important than my dating life." He rubbed the back of his neck. "Mark kind of..."

I groaned and turned around in frustration before facing him again. "Mark needs to stop intervening."

He blinked. "I'm sure he does it only because he cares."

I knew that, but it didn't help the frustration still coursing through me, knowing he had talked to Ethan behind my back. "And he said what?"

"That you've been scorned a time or two. I understand

147

what that's like, but I really hope that you will give me the chance to prove to you that I *am* different." He stepped forward, closing the gap between us, and lowered his voice to say, "I really like you, Astrid. More than I thought I did. Please give me the chance to prove to you that you are worth my time and effort."

I scoffed. "And what makes me worth your time? I have no experience being a mother. You don't even know if your daughter will like me or how I will treat her. So how can you make such a bold claim?"

"Because of how you talked about your own childhood. Your hopes to be better tell me that you are willing to grow and learn. Hell, *I'm* still learning. I'm not a perfect parent, and I wouldn't expect anyone to be. Sophia needs someone who will love her, and I know that you can do that. I know that you would be a good mom to her if we got that far. Even if we didn't, I just want to be able to have the chance to love you for as long as you are willing, because, Astrid, to me, you *are* worth that."

My breath caught in my throat. I had no response to that.

Within the next heartbeat, his lips were on mine. Hot. Desperate. Claiming. Passionate.

He pushed me up against the wall of safety deposit boxes, cushioning my head with a hand behind it. The cold biting of the metal was invigorating, and I felt my insides melt at his touch as he slid a hand around my waist to pull me close. He was so deliciously hard, his cock pressing into my abdomen and making my core clench.

The hand behind my head curled into my hair, pulling my head gently to the side as he began to trail kisses down my neck. I gasped as quietly as I could, still very aware that we were at work, in the vault, where anyone could walk in at any moment once they realized we were missing. It only added to the thrill of the moment.

His hand on my waist began to glide down along my hip to the hem of my skirt. I felt myself getting wet with awareness as his hand barely touched my bare thigh, as if asking permission. I didn't stop him. I couldn't. I didn't want to.

When I made no moves to stop him, he slipped his hand beneath my skirt and up between my thighs. It made a slow trail up, up, up. My breath quickened in response, my heart hammering in my chest.

I was locked in. One of his hands still gripped my hair, and the other was now just a breath away from my center. My clit tingled in anticipation while my wetness seeped into the thong I was wearing. He nipped lightly on my neck, and I gasped, barely containing the moan that threatened to escape.

Then a finger caressed the lining of my thong, barely brushing against my clit as it slipped to my vagina, and I couldn't help the small moan that slipped past my lips. He growled quietly against my collarbone in response, just as he pressed a finger into me.

"Fuck, you're so wet for me," he murmured against my throat.

I couldn't respond even if I wanted to because he was now curving his finger inside me, hitting that spot that made me squirm as pressure began to build from within. Then he pulled it out. I whimpered quietly at the loss, only to try to hold back another moan as he pushed two inside.

"Oh, fuck," I gasped.

"You like that, my star?" he asked.

I nearly convulsed at the sudden pet name. It only made it that much harder not to let loose on the already barely contained constraint I had on my moans. He curved his fingers, pumping them in and out, driving my orgasm to the brink of explosion. I could feel my walls clenching down around him.

"Ethan," I gasped. "I'm going to—"

"Cum for me, baby. Let it go."

"But...they'll...hear..."

He pumped harder and faster while adding his thumb to circle my clit. Just as I reached the precipice, his mouth swallowed my moans of pleasure as I fell over the edge. The only thing holding me up was his hand between my thighs and his body pressing mine against the wall of safety boxes. Once I had stopped shaking, he pulled his fingers out slowly and kissed me softly.

"That was the hottest thing I've ever seen," he whispered before beginning to kiss me again.

Then I heard his belt clank as it hit the floor.

"Ethan, they could—"

I was silenced by his lifting me and pinning me against the wall, his cock aimed and ready, with me just hovering over it.

"They could what?" he asked.

"They could walk in at any moment."

His smirk sent my insides aflame with desire. "Then we'd better make this quick."

He began to guide himself into me slowly. The feeling of him stretching me and filling me made my eyes roll into the back of my head. He pressed himself in the last few inches, and the small jolt had me moaning quietly in pleasure. Then he was thrusting into me at a tortuously slow pace.

"That's not quick," I whispered in a breathy voice.

"It will be if I go any faster. You feel so good, star. Oh shit," he groaned.

I chuckled, but it was cut short as his pace began to quicken and become more erratic. I could hear someone outside the vault, but they passed by. My core clenched with the thought of almost getting caught, and I could feel another orgasm beginning to build.

"Oh fuck, Astrid," Ethan growled into my neck as he began to kiss that sweet spot between my shoulder and neck.

I was heading straight to the edge, and as I fell, my moans swallowed by another of his passionate kisses, he fell with me, both of us finding our release in the other. We broke apart, gasping for air and coated in a light sheen of sweat. He rested his forehead against mine, his eyes open and staring intensely into mine.

"That was the most irresponsible and reckless thing I've ever done," he admitted with a light chuckle.

He slowly pulled out and set me down just as the lights beamed back to life, and we heard the vault dials beginning to turn. We glanced at the door, then each other, quickly straightening ourselves out. Just as Ethan had moved to put some distance between us and leaned against the opposite wall, the vault door swung open to reveal Mark and our manager.

"There you two are!" Mark exclaimed, but I didn't miss the mischief in his eyes.

"I deeply apologize. When the power went out, we weren't able to get into the vault. Are you two alright?" Lola asked.

"Fine now," I commented, trying to sound bored.

Mark quirked a brow, and I gave a slight nod, which made him smile before walking away. I had a sneaking suspicion that he was the reason we had gotten locked in to begin with. I'd have to question him about it later. And thank him...

Introductions

ETHAN

After being locked in the vault, I made the decision I wasn't going to let Astrid slip through my fingers ever again. Even though it was a heated, passionate moment, I knew that I had fallen hard for her and she was the one who was meant for me. Our bodies had fit together so perfectly, and after spending time getting to know her, I wanted to know her more. Indefinitely.

And I knew just how to ask her to be mine.

Valentine's Day was right around the corner.

I just needed to prepare.

I asked her out on a date following the vault lock-in, and thankfully, she agreed. Every weekend since then, we went out together. It was the weekend before Valentine's Day when I decided to finally introduce her to Sophia. I wanted to be sure Astrid was serious, and from the way conversations had been going and how well we connected during our dates, I knew now was the time. I approached her on Friday, eager to hear her thoughts.

"Hey, what do you think of a dinner and ice cream date

tonight with Sophia?" I asked in a hushed tone, keeping my eyes focused on the lobby.

I didn't miss her little gasp of surprise. It made my cock hard, and I positioned myself so that the barrier between her and Mark would hide it. She had no idea what her little sounds did to me, even after a month of dating.

"Uh, are you sure?" she inquired.

"Yes. I think it would be good for you two to meet officially. She keeps asking."

I chanced a glance at her, her warm brown eyes searching mine. She nodded.

"Alright. If you think it's best."

I grinned. "Perfect. I was thinking of dining in at home. Does that work?"

"At...at your house?"

I nodded.

"Uh, yeah, sure. Okay."

"Great."

Later that night, the doorbell rang.

"She's here!" Sophia yelled, followed by Rosy barking and the patter of running feet.

They skid around the corner together as I opened the door, revealing Astrid. I grabbed onto Rosy's collar just before she tried to leap up.

"Sorry about that. We are still working on not jumping on people. Rosy, down," I rushed out as I pulled the excited pup back.

Astrid giggled as she walked in. "That's alright."

"Hi! I'm Sophia!" Sophia greeted as she stood with her hands held in front of her, beaming a mile-wide smile. "You must be Astrid. Daddy's told me a lot about you, and I'd really like to be your friend. Can you be my friend? I'm six years old, and I really like to play with dolls. Do you like to play with dolls? Daddy said that—"

"Honey, let Astrid answer you before you ask more questions," I chuckled.

Astrid laughed and knelt to Sophia's level, taking her hand in hers. "Hi, Sophia. It's very nice to meet you. I would *love* to be your friend and play dolls with you. Who's your favorite doll?"

"I'll go get her!" She ran back to her room, leaving Astrid and me laughing in her wake.

"She seems excited," Astrid commented.

"Perhaps a little," I replied, releasing Ruby.

Our eyes met, and I felt that pull towards her. Giving in, I wrapped my arms around her, feeling her melt into me. I pecked her on the forehead just as Sophia came rushing back.

"Here she is! She's an Elsa doll," Sophia explained as she held up the Frozen-inspired Barbie doll. "And this is my other favorite. She's Belle."

"I see that. Belle is my favorite Disney princess. I'm guessing yours is Elsa," Astrid replied as she pulled away from me.

Sophia nodded, her eyes lit with joy. "She is! My whole *room* is pink, though. Because that's my favorite color. But my bed is Frozen. And I have a *giant* Olaf!"

"Do you? That's so cool."

Ruby barked at us, feeling ignored.

"Sophia, why don't you take Ruby outside for a bit?" I suggested.

"Okay!"

They ran off, and I sighed, feeling slightly bad for

throwing Astrid into the mix. I hadn't prepped her for how much energy the two had. Glancing at her, though, I could see her smiling as she watched them. She turned my way, giving me another smile.

"She's adorable," she commented.

"Very excited. I'm sorry. She can get a little... chaotic," I said as I rubbed the back of my neck.

"All kids are. That's why they bring such light into our lives even in the darkest moments."

My heart warmed at her words. She had no idea. Before Astrid, some days it had felt like the only reason I kept going was because of Sophia. She was the light of my life and the very reason I hadn't given up on love entirely. Her energy, unconditional love, and joy were what convinced me that someone could still be out there for us. And I was glad I hadn't given up.

"Yes, that they are," I replied with a smile. "Are you hungry?"

I led the way to the kitchen, grabbing out some cookware for pasta. Astrid sat at the barstool across from me.

"Well, you did promise me dinner," she joked.

"That I did." I chuckled.

"Astrid! Come play dolls with me!" Sophia chimed in as she ran inside.

"Do you need help with dinner?" Astrid asked me as she began to get off the stool, Sophia tugging her hand.

"No. You two go have fun," I said, feeling like I was offering her up as a sacrifice.

She nodded, then followed Sophia down the hall to her room, my daughter's excited voice chattering away. I shook my head. I really hoped that Astrid and Sophia would bond as much as Astrid and I had. It would really solidify in my mind everything I already felt I knew in my heart.

While the pasta boiled, I spread garlic butter on some French bread and popped it in the oven. Then I set to work making homemade Alfredo sauce and grilling the chicken. I was lucky to have a stove top that had a grill attachment that I easily slid into place. After seasoning the chicken, I placed it on the grill and began whisking together freshly grated Parmesan with butter and heavy cream. Once everything was done, I mixed it all together and plated it, adding a garnish of parsley on top of the pasta.

Instead of my usual calling out to Sophia, I decided to see how they interacted. I slipped down the hall quietly, their voices carrying louder to me as I approached.

"Oh, no! The giant snowman is coming after Belle," Sophia cried out.

"Oh dear! She's running away. Ahhh," Astrid replied. "And, what's this. A small, friendly snowman has appeared. 'Hi, I'm Olaf.'"

Sophia giggled.

"'And I like warm hugs. Can you hug me?' Belle hugs the snowman. 'Do you know where we can hide? There's a giant snowman chasing me!'"

Sophia roars, and I hear something being banged on the ground. I peered around the corner to see her holding her large Olaf up as she stomped toward where Astrid was holding the Belle doll and a smaller version of Olaf.

"'Follow me,'" Astrid says, having the two run towards Sophia's Frozen castle.

I chuckled. "Having fun?"

They both looked up, Sophia in joy and Astrid in surprise as an adorable blush formed on her cheeks.

"A blast!" Sophia cried out, jumping up. "Is dinner ready? I'm *starving*."

"Yes, it's ready," I said, then turned to Astrid. "Hope you like Alfredo."

"Love it," Astrid replied just as Sophia exclaimed, "Yay! Alfredo!"

I helped Astrid up off the floor as we chuckled and followed Sophia back to the dining room.

"Oh, wow. This looks... Is that homemade?" Astrid asked.

I nodded as I pulled out her chair for her.

"Daddy makes the *best* Alfredo," Sophia chimed in.

"Can't wait to try it," Astrid replied.

I sat down next to her across from Sophia. "Well, with that kind of review, I hope it lives up to expectations."

Sophia dove right in, taking a bite and smiling. "It's yummy!"

Astrid took a bite and closed her eyes, seeming to melt with it. "Oh my goodness, Ethan. This is fabulous!"

I flushed. "Well, thank you. I'm glad you like it."

"Does your dad cook like this every night?" Astrid asked of Sophia.

"Not *every* night. Sometimes we just do mac 'n' cheese with hot dogs or frozen pizza," she replied as she took another bite. "He likes to cook, though."

"Lucky you!"

"Do *you* like to cook?"

"Sometimes. But I don't really have anyone to cook for, so I usually order out or make a salad."

"That sounds sad."

Astrid chuckled. "It's not so bad. I have a cat, and she keeps me company."

"But a cat doesn't talk."

"Well, she meows at me like she's talking."

Sophia giggled. "That's silly."

"Sounds like quite the character," I commented.

"She can be. She has a lot of sass, that's for sure," Astrid replied.

"Can we meet her?" Sophia asked.

"Maybe someday," Astrid replied with a smile. "That's up to your dad."

"Perhaps in a couple of weeks," I answered before Sophia could question again.

After dinner, Astrid helped me wash the dishes in the kitchen while Sophia got ready for bed. We decided to watch a movie while eating our ice cream, which would make it late in the evening for Sophia. Plus, we argued that it would be cozier for her if she were in PJs. She reluctantly agreed.

"Sophia is truly adorable," Astrid commented as she put away the last dish, then folded the towel and hung it on the oven's handle next to the other rag. "And has quite the imagination."

"That she does. I hope she wasn't too much," I commented.

"Not at all."

I scooted closer to her. "So, she won't scare you away?"

She shook her head as she gazed up at me. "No."

It came out breathy. Quiet. Her eyes heated as I closed the gap between us, pinning her against the cabinets with my arms on either side of her on the countertop.

"I hope you're not just saying that, because I'm falling for you, Astrid," I murmured.

Her breath hitched, making my blood pulse skyrocket within in an instant.

I nuzzled against her neck. "Am I too much?"

I felt her shake her head as she whispered, "No."

I wrapped a hand around her waist to pull her closer, my cock throbbing against her pelvis, making me only want more of her.

"I-I'm falling, too, Ethan," she said, half moan, half whisper.

I pulled back and searched her eyes, seeing just how deep she was falling from just the way she gazed back at me.

"You've been so kind. Gentle. Patient. And understanding. I haven't had that in a very long time." She looked down at her hands on my chest. "I didn't realize how fast I had been falling for you until tonight."

I got lost in her brown eyes as she looked back up at me.

"I think I might even be in—"

"Ready!" Sophia exclaimed as she came around the corner.

I immediately backed away from Astrid, putting some space between us and turning to adjust myself while playing it off as getting the bowls down.

"Let's go find a movie to watch," Astrid said.

She touched my hand gently before following Sophia out to the living room.

"No Frozen!" I hollered after them as I pulled out the ice cream from the freezer.

I heard Sophia groan in disappointment.

"How about Brave? Have you seen that one yet?" Astrid asked.

"Yeah! Brave!" Sophia agreed.

I sighed. At least it wasn't Frozen.

After Bedtime

ASTRID

SOPHIA FELL ASLEEP IN THE LAST FIFTEEN MINUTES of the movie. She looked like an angel sleeping cradled up to Ethan's chest, and I could feel my heart swell at the sight of them together. He was clearly a loving and devoted father to her, which only made me fall for him even more.

I berated myself internally again for almost having spilled how deeply I had already fallen for him. We had only known each other for two months now. Surely I couldn't be in love with him already?

But I was.

I couldn't explain why. Or how. But somehow, I had fallen deeply, irrevocably in love with this man. It baffled me.

I blamed it on the close proximity in our situation. We spent every day at work together. On the weekends, since our little heated exchange in the vault, we went on at least one date, sometimes two. It just felt...right to be around him. I never would have guessed I would fall in love with him, but here I was.

Sophia sighed in her sleep as Ethan adjusted himself to pick her up carefully. I smiled at him as he tenderly carried her back to her room. A few minutes went by before he returned, bringing a bottle of wine and some glasses with him.

"Want some?" he asked.

"Sure," I replied, sitting up a little more and moving the blanket back over my legs.

He poured us a couple of glasses before sitting next to me, draping his arm over my shoulders and pulling me close. His warmth seeped into me, pooling low in my core. I blushed, loving the feel of it but also slightly embarrassed at how easily he could turn me on. Was it the novelty of our relationship? Or something else? I couldn't recall ever feeling this way about anyone, even a couple of months into a relationship. After the first initial week or so, things petered off. They became... comfortable. Boring, almost. Ethan was anything but. My attraction to him went deeper than just the surface.

He began to stroke my shoulder casually, the sensation sending a chill down my spine.

"Are you cold?" he asked.

"No," I replied.

"Would you like to watch something else?"

"Hm, I'm okay with just sitting and talking."

"Alright. What would you like to talk about?"

"Well, for starters, I had a wonderful time tonight."

He sighed. "But?"

I sat up and quirked a brow at him. "No 'but'. I had a great time, and I'm glad I finally got to meet Sophia." I chewed my lip. "Do you think she liked me?"

He chuckled. "*Liked* you? I think she *adored* you. About as much as I do."

I blushed and looked away until his hand caressed my cheek and turned me back to face him. My breath hitched when I realized how close he was, our lips only a breath apart.

"Why did you look away?" he asked quietly.

"I'm just... not used to *this*."

"This?"

"Being adored."

"Astrid?"

I looked up into his eyes instead of his lips. "Hm?"

"I don't just adore you."

I blinked. "Wh-what do you mean?"

"I think I'm in love with you."

I stopped breathing. My heart hammered in my chest. Butterflies flew wildly in my stomach while my core heated with desire.

"I think I'm in love with you, too," I whispered.

I barely had time to set my glass down on the table beside us as his lips pressed gently against mine and his hand moved from my cheek to the nape of my neck, drawing me closer. He leaned over me, pushing me further onto the couch, as he placed his glass on the table next to mine. He laid me down gently, making sure I had enough room to move as he positioned himself above me, with a leg between mine. I moaned softly as a hand slid beneath my shirt to cradle my breast.

A flashback of Asher went through my head, but I shoved it down hard and fast. Ethan was different. Gentle, but passionate. Never forceful. Kind. And oh—

His hand pinched my nipple and rolled it between his fingers, sending waves of sensation directly to my already sensitive clit. I arched beneath him, a gasp for air escaping me. His lips began to trail along my neck to my collarbone, pausing to nibble and gently suck on the spot that drove me absolutely wild. I couldn't hold back the moan of pleasure it drew from me.

"Fuck I love the sounds you make," he growled against my skin, sending prickles of awareness through me. "They drive me absolutely insane."

He thrust against me, letting me feel precisely what they do to him.

"And your little gasps. Fucking hell, star. They will be my undoing one day."

He drew such a gasp from me as he nipped at the spot on my neck between shoulder and collarbone. My hands gripped his shoulders in desperation to pull him closer. I needed him over all of me. I wanted to feel the weight of him, but he aggravatingly held himself inches above me. Close, but not close enough.

"Ethan," I whimpered.

"Tell me what you want."

"You." It came out breathy when he rolled my nipples between his fingers again. "I-I want y-you."

My back arched again of its own volition in response to his mouth suddenly wrapped around my other nipple, his teeth lightly grazing over it. He sucked on it gently at first, drawing it in, making it harden. Then he sucked a little harder, testing how far I could take it. When his teeth gently bit, I fought the yelp of surprise, not wanting to wake Sophia.

"Ethan, I wouldn't do that," I said breathlessly.

"And why not?" he asked as he looked up at me, his hair tousled.

"I can't promise I'll be quiet if you do that."

His grin was wicked. "You'll have to try your best to be."

"Ethan-"

I didn't have time to say anything more as he bit down gently on my nipple again. I covered my mouth as I moaned loudly.

"I'm just getting started with you," he commented. "But I think you'd be more comfortable in the bedroom."

I blushed and nodded.

The absence of his weight above me made me want to pull him back down, but before I could react, he was picking me up beneath my legs. I gasped in shock, wrapping my arms around his neck for support. He chuckled, the sound vibrating against my side, then began to walk down the hall to his room.

His bedroom was cozy, already lit by a warm, amber glow that softened the dark and illuminated a bed with a moss-green quilt. I didn't have time to take in much more before I was laid on the bed and he was on top of me again, kissing me feverishly. He tasted like wine, sweet and intoxicating. I wanted to drown in it.

His knee brushed against the apex between my thighs, providing just enough friction that I fought not to rub myself against him. A hand slid to the hem of my pants, slowly undoing the button of my jeans, then pulling the zipper down. I could feel the wetness on my underwear, hot and ready for him, without his evening touching my most sensitive area. His kisses were relentless, stealing my breath away as his hand slid between my jeans and underwear, dipping into my wetness. He groaned into my mouth as his finger pressed slightly against me, teasing my entrance.

I whimpered, needing more.

He responded by removing his hand, and I pouted, my eyebrows furrowing. He pulled away, leaving me panting, and began to kiss down my body. Pausing to give my nipples a quick nip each, he alternated between delicate kisses and playful nips, the effect ratcheting up my desire and need. He paused just above the hem of my jeans to slowly pull them down, leaving me in just my underwear. I chanced a glance down to see him looking me over with appraisal.

"You are so fucking beautiful, star," he told me as our eyes met. "And I can't wait to pleasure your body."

I shivered with longing at his words.

He knelt at the end of the bed and wrapped his arms around my legs, pulling me down to him. The way he gazed at me only made my core clench even more, eager and antici-pating his next move. His hands slid down my thighs, goosebumps following in their wake. Then they slipped beneath my ass and grabbed my underwear, pulling them off as his hands continued downward.

"Mm, I can't wait to taste you," he murmured.

Fucking hell. He was going so slow. Too slow. I was already hot and ready for him. Yet, I didn't want to rush him. I was enjoying this new form of torture. My body was feverish for him.

His hands began a languid pace up my calves as he placed kisses on the inside of them, trailing upward to the back of my knees, then back down along my inner thighs, spreading me open like a buffet. His hot breath lingered over me, my clit tingling in longing to be touched, soothed, teased. *Something.* I squirmed slightly, needing friction before I burst.

The instant his tongue touched me, I was arching my back, and my eyes rolled into the back of my head. I moaned deeply as he flicked it over my clit. I gripped the sheets tightly as he continued the slow full-tongue to flick motion, leisurely drawing out the sensation of my body getting what it wanted but still needing more. I could feel the coil within tightening each time, seeking to be let loose, yet he wasn't going fast enough. I needed *more.*

"Ethan," I gasped. "Please."

His finger teased my entrance, dipping in just slightly as he licked again, but this time circled my clit. Then his mouth was gone. His finger hovering.

"Please what, star?" he asked, his voice playful.

I whimpered. "I need more."

His finger began to ease inside of me. "You are so wet already. I can feel your walls clenching."

I panted, unable to respond.

"You like it when I take my time with you, don't you?"

I nodded, moaning as he curled his finger and pressed against my G-spot.

He held it there as he began to circle my clit with his tongue again, at first going slow, then gradually increasing his rhythm. As he did, he began to pump his finger in and out of me. As I could feel my orgasm building impossibly more, he slipped a second finger in, spreading me from the inside.

I couldn't take it anymore. I was about to explode. I could feel myself clenching so tightly around him that he could barely move his fingers out, instead opting for curling and uncurling his fingers. Just as I thought I couldn't possibly get any more tightly wound, it let loose.

My orgasm had me screaming, his mouth quickly swallowing the sound as my body convulsed involuntarily, his hand still pumping in and out. As I came down, gasping for air, he retracted his fingers and grinned down at me.

"Damn, that was hot," he whispered.

"I hope... I didn't..." I started.

"You didn't. I promise she's still asleep."

I pushed him back. "My turn."

I continued to push him until I was off the bed, then I turned him and shoved, causing him to fall back. He smirked at me.

"Aggressive are we?" he asked.

I snorted and knelt before him, taking his cock into my hands. I stroked him, using the precum at the tip as lubricant until it became sticky. Then I took him into my mouth, easing him in and giving him the slow, deliberate torture he had given me. His hand wrapped into my hair, holding me but not forcing me down. I bobbed my head, hollowing out my cheeks, and taking him all in each time.

"Oh, fuck," he growled, his grip tightening as he fought not to lose control.

I picked up the pace, cupping his balls in one hand and supporting myself on the bed with the other. He lost control after that, holding my head steady with a tight grip on my hair as he began to thrust into my mouth. I moaned around him, letting the vibrations travel up my throat and making him groan. Then he yanked me away and up to him, kissing me wildly before pulling me into his lap.

He rammed into me, hard and deep. I gasped and moaned at the same time. His pace wasn't slow anymore, but he was thrusting into me with wild abandon. He tore my shirt off, and I quickly undid my bra, never losing the rhythm of his cock pounding into me. His mouth immediately clamped onto my nipple as soon as it bounced free. My head fell back in pure bliss as I steadied myself with my hands on his chest.

I could feel myself dangerously close to orgasm again. My core clenched around his cock, the feel sublime.

Before he could cum, he flipped us over and stood at the edge of the bed, hands gripping my hips. His pace became erratic, thrusting harder and faster. I needed more. I pulled my leg up and threw it over his shoulder. He groaned, kissing my calf, his grip on my hips tightening.

"Ethan, I'm going to—" I gasped.

"Cum for me, baby," he growled.

And we both found our release together, moaning and groaning as his cock pulsed inside of me, drawing out my orgasm.

Then he pulled me up into the bed with him, exhaustion overcoming me. As my eyes began to drift closed, I heard him whisper, "I love you, Astrid."

Be Mine

ETHAN

Astrid fell asleep quickly after we finished ravaging each other. I had planned to take my time with her tonight, but when she had gone down on me... Holy fuck, her mouth sent me to heaven. I couldn't contain myself any longer after that. I'd needed her body like I needed air. There was just no way I would have been able to hold out any longer without cumming. Which I had wanted to do inside her, not out on the floor or on the bed. Maybe another time, but not tonight. Tonight I wanted her to feel worshiped, valued, and cherished.

I pulled the blankets over us before drifting off, hoping I had done as much.

The next morning, Rosy's wet nose pressing into my cheek woke me a moment before Sophia came in. Astrid rolled over in her sleep before blearily blinking her eyes and tightening the blanket around her.

"Astrid stayed the night?" Sophia asked innocently.

"Uh, yeah. It got really late, and I didn't want her driving home in the dark," I bluffed. "Can you take Rosy outside to go potty, please? We will be out in just a second to make you some breakfast."

"Okay! C'mon, Rosy." She ran off, the pup trailing behind her.

"I am *so* sorry," Astrid blurted, immediately jumping from the bed to search for her clothes.

"For what?" I asked as I stretched the last bits of sleep from my body.

"I shouldn't have stayed. I should have gone home so she wouldn't question you."

I chuckled as I got up and pulled her into a hug. "It's fine. Honestly."

Her eyes were wide with indecision and fear.

I tucked a piece of hair behind her ear. "Go take a shower and relax. I promise, everything is fine." I kissed her temple. "I'll start on breakfast."

She nodded, then headed to my bathroom. I waited until the shower was running before going out to the kitchen. I was pulling out pancake mix when Sophia came back inside.

"Hey, kiddo. Can I talk to you for a second?" I asked.

"What's up, Daddy?" she asked, sidling up next to me.

I picked her up and set her on the counter so we would be at eye level. "Do you like Astrid?"

She nodded.

"Good. What do you think about her coming over more often?"

"To play dolls with me?"

"Well, yes, and to spend time with us."

She nodded again, her eyes lit with excitement. "I want that!"

"Okay. But shh. Don't say anything yet, okay?"

"Okay."

"Alright. Go get dressed while I make pancakes."

She skipped down the hall, and I grinned. Now I just had to ask Astrid. I would wait, though. I had a plan, and everything was following it smoothly. Just a couple more days until I could act on it. Leora had already agreed to watch Sophia, so I didn't need to worry about that. I only worried about what Astrid would say.

Valentine's Day arrived, and I couldn't be more anxious but excited at the same time. It landed on a Wednesday, unfortunately, but that was alright. I would make it work, so long as Astrid agreed. I approached her in the last hour before closing time.

"Are you busy tonight?" I asked.

"Well, no, of course not," she commented, almost sounding annoyed.

I quirked a brow. "Everything alright?"

"Yeah, fine."

She didn't sound fine. I hesitated, then asked, "Can you come with me after work?"

"Sure."

I nodded, then went to make sure I had everything wrapped up for the day. I was confused by her behavior. Everything had seemed fine all day. Maybe she had gotten a bad customer towards the end of the day, and I hadn't noticed. Or perhaps she was getting her period. That would throw a wrench in things. No matter. I would make it work.

I waited for her by my truck. She was talking to Mark as she came out of the bank, then headed toward me after hugging him. She still looked upset, and I hoped I could find out why before we got back to my house.

"Do you want to drop your car off at home first?" I asked.

"Yeah, I probably should," she replied.

"I'll follow you."

After dropping her car off, she got in my truck, seeming tense.

"Is everything alright, Astrid? You seem annoyed," I asked hesitantly.

"I'm fine," she replied.

Okay... I took a deep breath. If she didn't want to tell me, then I wouldn't push her. I pulled into the garage, then went around to open her door and help her down. I could feel my excitement ramping up, despite her mood. I just hoped everything would still go as planned.

I let her lead the way.

She paused when she opened the door leading to the house, and I fought the grin on my face. Candlelight bounced off the walls, glowing softly in the hallway. The scent of rose petals wafted toward us. She spun, tears in her eyes.

"I thought..." she stopped to sniffle. "I thought you had forgotten the day."

I quirked a brow at her. "A romantic like me forgetting the most romantic day of the year?" I shook my head, chuckling. "Is that why you were upset?"

She looked down and nodded.

I turned her head upward with a finger beneath her chin. "Never."

I nodded toward the house, urging her on. She turned back around and walked inside, following the path I had laid for her to the living room, where a large teddy bear sat on the couch with a big heart saying "Be Mine". On the coffee table was a bottle of wine and two glasses, already laid out for us with some chocolates. She gasped, her hand flying toward her mouth.

"Ethan," she murmured, turning back around.

"Astrid, I was serious when I told you I love you," I told her, fighting to maintain my distance. "And I know we have only been dating a few short months, but..." I got down on a knee and pulled out the ring I'd been saving. "Will you marry me? Not right away, but you know, when you're ready."

She laughed, tears flowing down her cheeks as she nodded quickly. "Oh my... Yes! Yes, yes, yes!"

She flung herself at me, her arms wrapping around me and nearly choking me. As she pulled away, I slipped the ring onto her finger and kissed her, feeling my heart explode with pure joy for the first time in years.

A Note from Hazel

If you made it to the end, thank you for giving *Vaulted* a chance.

It is readers like you who make a difference and truly make indie author publishing worth it. I would really appreciate it if you left a review on your favorite review platform to encourage me and help other readers know what to expect and make an informed decision about whether this book is right for them.

Writing a book is a lot of work, but reading your reviews makes it all worth it!

I'd also *love* to hear from you! Feel free to reach out to me on social media (authorhazelwilder).

XOXO,

Hazel

Acknowledgments

First, I would like to thank everyone who has stayed on the journey with me for this series. Your love, dedication, and support carry me through, and I cannot express my gratitude to you enough. Thank you so much for being there for me, helping me develop my craft, and encouraging me to move forward.

Thank you so much to my husband, who encourages me and inspires some of the...spicier scenes. ;) I'm one lucky gal to have you in my life.

Thank you SO MUCH to my beta and ARC readers, whose names I won't disclose for privacy reasons. You are all amazing, and I appreciate you pointing out inconsistencies, or the time when Astrid decided to wear the whole closet in chapter one. I appreciate you pointing out when my brain goes faster than my hands and reminding me to slow down - it will get there! This book would not be what it is without you all and your support.

A huge thank you to my Lovers Ream member: Jen. I love your excitement for my books and your support throughout the writing process. And your patience when I throw in the occasional plot-twist. ;)

Finally, if you read this book, I hope you fell in love with Astrid and Ethan, almost as much as I did. Their story was inspired by real-life events, but with a fantastical flair, if you catch my drift. You have my eternal gratitude for taking a chance on this book. So, thank you!

Until the next!
XOXO,
Hazel

About the Author

HAZEL WILDER lives in the wild, beautiful state of Alaska. While she may not run into wolves every day, there is just something so wild about where she lives that inspires the Pine Valley Wolves series. Lovers of Brantley is inspired by realistic scenarios and stories she has heard over the years, with a little extra flair and spice. When she's not writing, you can find her spending time with family or crocheting.

Find more information on her website www.authorhazelwilder.com or follow her on social media at:

instagram.com/authorhazelwilder

tiktok.com/@authorhazelwilder

reamstories.com/loversofbrantley

Also by Hazel Wilder

Lovers of Brantley Series

Sweet Dreams, Lover Boy

Dream On, Boss Man

Oven Mitts and Mistletoe

Vault

Pine Valley Wolves

Rebel

www.ingramcontent.com/pod-product-compliance
Lightning Source LLC
Chambersburg PA
CBHW060156130626
46556CB00006B/2659